DOTTY

and the Chimney Thief

Emma Warner-Reed

First published by Calendar House Press 2016

Cover design by Emma Warner-Reed

Designed and Typeset by Emma Warner-Reed

The DOTTY Series Vol. 2 – DOTTY and the Chimney Thief

Summary:

All is not well in the world of The Calendar House. There's a rogue sweep on the loose, and they're not just stealing trinkets from the houses they enter, they're stealing the chimneys, too! To add insult to injury, Little Joe Raman from the corner shop on Dotty's beloved Wyvern Road has gone missing and nobody knows why.

Has Joe been abducted by thieves, or is there another reason for his disappearance? And can Dotty stop the Chimney Thief, before all the portals into the world of the ordinary folk have been sealed forever?

ISBN: 978-0-9955662-0-0

For the Curly Crew.

CONTENTS

Contents

Prologue

A Robbery

It was cloudy and the moon was nowhere to be seen in the sky. A house stood at the end of a deserted close, seemingly empty, its inhabitants sleeping soundly through the quietest part of the night. They were in too deep a slumber to be disturbed by a rustle in the drawing room, or to be alarmed when first a boy and then a huge black-and-white bird appeared on the hearth. Cautiously the pair scanned the room for signs of movement. Then, establishing that all was quiet, they set to work.

"Check all the drawers," directed the boy, as they searched the room. The boy looked about fifteen years old, although he was small for his age. Ragged and covered in soot, his bare feet left dirty marks on the carpet as they worked.

The bird squawked a finding.

"What is it, Mordecai?" asked the boy, crossing the room to look. The bird had found a tray full of small silver snuff boxes laid neatly in a drawer. The boy rifled through the drawer carelessly, scattering the boxes hither and thither. "Nah," he said. "These aren't what we are after, pretty though they might be. The King said we are searching for a locket: gold, inlaid with emeralds and seed pearls." He closed the drawer. "Come on, we've got a lot of ground to cover tonight."

The bird eyed the drawer hungrily.

"Come on." The boy tugged at the bird's wing. "Great greedy magpies. And don't even think about taking one, all right? Master's orders."

The boy walked back to the open fire, the bird trailing behind a little, one eye still on the drawer. Once safely within the confines of the chimney opening the boy crouched down, producing something small and delicate from his pocket, harnessed inside the skeleton of a leaf. "Ready?" he asked his accomplice.

The bird nodded.

The boy opened his hand, gently blowing across the object and out into the room. "Magick be mine," he whispered, and within a wink, bird and boy were gone.

When the inhabitants of the house awoke early the following morning, they would discover that they had been the victims of some sort of strange practical joke, in which what appeared to be a barefooted child and a giant bird had danced around their drawing room with blackened dirty feet. Perhaps even more bizarrely, they would also find that the pranksters had blocked up their fireplace with such skill it was as if the hearth had never been there.

On speaking to the police, the couple would at first say they thought that nothing had been taken from the upturned room. But on closer inspection, they would come to realise that a single silver snuff box was curiously missing from a drawer.

A Robbery

Chapter 1

Missing!

In which Sylv tells Dotty about Joe's disappearance and Gobby scolds the dog

The familiar image of Dotty's best friend looked out at her from the iPad. Sylv's bottom lip trembled, and her complexion was ashen. Dotty didn't ever think she'd seen Sylv looking so upset.

"Oh my word, what's happened?" Dotty asked. "Are you okay?"

"Can you come now, Dot? Can you just come to Cardiff? Please! I need your help."

Dotty looked exasperated. "Is it your homework again? Look, you know I can't come hopping down the chimney every time you call. It's just not practical."

"It's not homework, it's Joe. He's...well, he's *vanished*!" Sylv's bottom lip quivered more violently, and she broke into a sob.

"Vanished? What do you mean, 'vanished'? Are you sure?"

"Yes I'm sure." Sylv looked cross. "He's gone missing. Plain disappeared. Look, Dot, I really need you to come. Right now."

"Okay, I'm coming. What have the police said?"

"That's the thing," wailed Sylv. "The police don't seem to know anything. They can't explain what happened. Joe went missing from his bedroom but he sleeps on the top floor and you can only get to his room by going through his sister, Jazz's. There are a couple of skylights in the roof, but they're way too small even for Joe to climb through, and you know how small he is. Jazz swears that she was in her bedroom all night and that she never saw him. But without walking past her there's just no other way he could have got out."

Dotty waited as her friend paused for a moment, convulsing with sobs, trying to catch her breath.

"The police are saying either he must have run away or, worse, that his family's disappeared him! But of course that's not true. It can't be. Oh Dot, it's terrible. Joe's dad's awful upset."

Dotty tried to think of what her mam used to say to her when she was crying. "Okay Sylv, now take some deep breaths," Dotty soothed, using the most reassuring grown-up voice she could muster. "It's awful about Joe, of course it is. But if the police can't work it out, what do you think *I* can do?"

"Isn't it obvious?" Sylv replied, her tense, pale face staring up from the screen. "The police don't know all the facts, do they? I mean, if he didn't go out through the door, he must have left another way – like up the chimney."

Dotty inhaled sharply, shocked. It hadn't occurred to her that a sweep might be involved. A rogue sweep, even. This was the worst kind of news. Her mind raced with possibilities.

"Oh Dot, you've just got to come," Sylv moaned. "I need you here now. You're my best friend. Come on *butt*[1], I know you can help. Puhleeeaase! I want you here with me so we can figure this out together."

In truth, Dotty had been on board since she heard the word 'chimney'. "All right, Sylv, I said I'm coming, didn't I? But just hang on until after dinner, can you? Gobby'll go nuts if I miss my tea. You know what she's like."

"Yeah, okay," Sylv conceded with a sniff.

"Right, then," Dotty instructed. "Just sit tight. I'm on my way."

*

---

[1] Welsh for "friend".

The supper bell trilled impatiently in the distance. It was the cook, Mrs Gobbins (affectionately named 'Gobby' by the girls), calling her for tea.

Dotty's life had changed so much over the last year or so that it seemed almost impossible now to remember the way things had been before. She still felt like the same feisty little Welsh girl inside, but since the tragic loss of her parents last November, everything was different. Her old life back in Cardiff seemed a world and a half away. The accident had made the news.

"Local Couple Die with Family Pets in House Fire. Daughter Narrowly Escapes Blaze."

Dotty was haunted by memories of that night. If only she hadn't nagged Mam and Dad to have a firework party in the back garden of their small, suburban home. She remembered how excited she and Sylv had been, running home from school that afternoon, giggling and laughing. And she remembered with bittersweet regret how much effort her dad had put into the display, buying up every firework from Eddie Raman's Corner shop. Mr Raman's son, Joe, had taken great delight in telling the girls when they stopped in for sweets on their way home from school.

But now she needed to get to Cardiff and to Sylv. She had to help Joe, if she could. The cross-sounding bell continued to ting-a-ling in the background, calling her impatiently. Dotty tutted to herself. Could she get away with it if she left right now? No, probably not. Gobby would go nuts if Dotty let her supper go cold.

Dotty gestured to a fat old brown-and-white spaniel that lay across the doorway, forming quite an effective draught excluder. "Come on, Geoff. Dinner time!"

Geoff jumped up eagerly, the years visibly dropping off him at the mention of food. Together the two hurtled down the back stairs that led into the kitchen.

"Sorry, Mrs Gobbins," Dotty apologised as she poked her head around the kitchen door, anticipating the roasting she was about to receive for being slow to answer the bell. She tried to look casual whilst attempting to hide Geoff's rather large outline behind her legs, only too aware of the cook's dislike of dogs in her precious kitchen.

The old cook was ladling homemade strawberry jam out of a vat of the stuff that teetered precariously on the corner of the dresser, slopping it into a smaller glass serving dish. As usual, she looked as if she had entered into a battle with the flour bin and lost. The ladle slipped out of her hands and landed back in the vat with a juicy *thwack*, splattering her with small sticky globules of jam. Together with the dusting of flour, it made her look like she had a severe case of strawberry jam measles. Dotty suppressed a giggle.

"And about time, too," Gobby snapped as she manhandled the glass lid back on to the oversized container. "I thought you were never coming! Well, tuck in, girl. There are ham sandwiches and toasted teacakes, and there's a nice slab of Christmas cake there. Oh," she stopped herself. "I forgot the cheese." She bustled off in the direction of the larder, covered in flour and spotted with jam. "There's a nice piece of Wensleydale (cheese) out back. I'll go fetch it."

"There's really no need, Mrs Gobbins, I..." she trailed off. Gobby was gone. Dotty had never understood the Yorkshire custom of eating fruit cake with a slice of cheese, or indeed of eating Christmas cake in March. Both seemed plain weird to her. But there was no point trying to change Gobby's mind once she had it set on something, so Dotty just let her put it on the table with the other tea things.

Dotty scooped up a plate, hurriedly filling it with food from the table that she did like. She needed to get to Sylv's. She grabbed a couple of ham sandwiches for starters, the freshly-baked gammon spilling out of the soft homemade bread, butter dripping from them where the warmth of the meat had melted it. Her mouth watered. Despite her haste to leave, she was actually quite hungry. She spooned a couple of round, crunchy pickled onions out of a jar and onto her plate. "Want one, Geoff?" she teased the overweight spaniel.

Geoff grimaced visibly, and Dotty laughed as he sniffed rather more hopefully at the baked ham. She knew that Geoff hated pickled onions, although from experience she also knew that he wasn't past giving one a good suck if nothing better was on offer.

Dotty was about to make a swift exit when Gobby came whirling back into the room with a gigantic round of cheese in hand. She fought to find a place for it on the already-full farmhouse table. "There," she said, giving a satisfied nod. "That should be enough for a modest supper."

Dotty snorted, her mouth full of sandwich. Modest! This table had never seen modest.

"I'd better get Mr Winchester's tea tray ready. He'll be eating in his study tonight."

Dotty had never known Great Uncle Winchester to eat a meal anywhere *except* in his study. She raised an eyebrow in acknowledgement.

Gobby busied herself piling a tray high with sandwiches and teacakes, and fresh slices of Battenberg cake (one of the cook's specialities and Winchester's particular favourite). Then she set about warming the teapot on the great cast iron range, unearthing a tin of her employer's best gunpowder tea.

Dotty crammed her mouth full of sandwich, half sitting, half standing, as she tried to find an excuse to leave the table. Meanwhile Geoff skulked under the great scrubbed kitchen table top. Dotty suspected that he was waiting for the perfect moment to snaffle something from around the heavily laden table's edges. Although when Gobby took the tea tray out to her great uncle, the dog would have plenty of opportunity to steal a meaty snack.

"Well, that should do." Gobby gave a satisfied nod, surveying the heavily-laden tea tray.

"Why don't I take that?" asked Dotty, seeing her chance to escape.

"No, dear. You eat your supper. I'll call Mr Strake. Sit yourself back down dear."

Dotty had no choice but to oblige her. Gobby stepped neatly over to a small square panel on the kitchen wall and pressed one of the buttons. A bell rang in the distance. A moment passed and there was a cursory knock on the kitchen door. Not waiting for an answer, the door opened.

"You rang, Mrs Gobbins?" A tall, lanky figure stooped in the doorway. It was Strake. Dotty gave an involuntary shudder. Even if Gobby had not summoned him, instinct would have told Dotty it was her great uncle's personal secretary before she ever saw him. The man appeared to carry about with him an uncomfortable air. It wasn't anything Dotty could see, of course. Just a bad feeling that seemed to follow him, infecting everything Strake came into contact with. If it had been visible, Dotty imagined Strake would have been stalking around bearing a damp, dark brown fog of sorts on that unnaturally curved back of his.

Strake, likewise, seemed to resent Dotty's presence in the kitchen. He twitched, nervously. No discussion had ever taken place between them about his thwarted attempt to steal the Calendar House Key from Dotty and her friends; or of how his failure had been received by the villains that he had tried to steal it for: the awful rogue sweep traders, Porguss and Poachling. Dotty reckoned they must have given him a roasting! Whatever had happened, Strake seemed to fear her now and, Dotty had to admit, she wasn't displeased with the result.

Even months after the event, Dotty was still angry at the thought of what these three had tried to do – stealing the precious Calendar House Key, so long thought lost. And all so that they could use the ancient sweeps' magic to take innocent children from their beds, forcing them up the chimneys and away into a life of slavery in the cold, dark world of the sweeps. She glowered at Strake. He winced in reply.

You could have cut the atmosphere with a knife, although, as usual, Gobby seemed blissfully unaware of anything other than the nose in front of her face.

"Mr Strake, would you take Mr Winchester's tea tray in to him? I'm waiting on a batch of Welsh cakes, and I don't want them to burn."

Strake quickly resumed his usual superlative air. "Certainly, Mrs Gobbins: nothing is too much trouble for Mr Winchester, of course." He eyed Gobby, rather pointedly, Dotty thought, as if he were suggesting that her priorities should lay with her employer, rather than with her baking.

"Well, that's settled, then," she trilled. "You'd better hurry, Mr Strake, the tea will be getting cold. I've warmed the pot, but—"

Strake interrupted Gobby's speech by whisking the tray out of her hands with long, spidery fingers and, without another word, beating a hasty retreat out of the kitchen. He backed out of the doorway, as was customary for him. Dotty knew that he did this as a show of politeness or respect, but she couldn't help but think that Strake's real reason for not showing his back to the occupant of the room he was leaving was for fear that they might be unable to resist the urge to stick a knife in it.

No sooner had the air cleared of the unpleasant atmosphere caused by Strake's presence in the room, but another figure loomed at the rear kitchen door. It was Kenny, the gardener. Kenny cut an altogether different figure, leaning heavily on the door frame in his usual casual manner. He smelled of dirt and earth and old tobacco. Dotty liked Kenny. She beamed at his arrival.

"Hiya, Kenny," she mumbled through a mouthful of teacake.

"Hello, Miss Dotty," replied Kenny. His face remained serious but a twinkle in his eye gave away his affection for her. "Mrs Gobbins, have you seen, Geoff? I have orders for his bath."

Geoff flattened himself against the stone flag floor. Dotty watched the dog's vain attempt to make himself undetectable with amusement. Clearly he understood the word 'bath'.

"Certainly not, Kenneth. You know I don't allow dogs in my kitchen," Gobby snorted. She really didn't like dogs, and in particular Geoff, Dotty guessed on account of the fact that he was always stealing food out of the larder, or even off the kitchen table if he could get away with it.

Dotty shuffled impatiently, itching to get going. She really wanted to see Sylv now. She studied the floor, trying not to give away the spaniel's hiding place, but it didn't help. Kenny's sharp old eyes quickly spotted Geoff's brown and white paws poking out from beneath the tablecloth.

"Mrs Gobbins, I think you'll find he's under the table," he remarked wryly.

"Oh my legs and arms! That dog will be the death of me!" Gobby threw her flour covered hands dramatically into the air.

With two short strides, Kenny had the dog by the collar and was dragging him ungraciously out of his hiding place and the warmth of the kitchen, to his soapy fate at the mercy of the garden hose.

The cook turned to Dotty. "I assume you knew about this," she accused.

At last, Dotty had found the perfect moment to make herself scarce. Hastily, she made her excuses. "Right, Mrs Gobbins, I'm off to, er, *Skype* Sylv."

And before she could scold her any further, Dotty got down from the table and bid a hasty retreat back to her bedroom.

Once there, Dotty took a deep breath, holding the locket firmly in the palm of her hand, as was her habit. Her fingers enveloped the heavy gold lozenge, its sturdy chain still safely around her neck.

It wasn't that Dotty wasn't used to chimney travel by now. Dotty had travelled this way many times since the events leading up to last Christmas and her discovery of the Calendar House Key: a magical locket that her dear departed mother had buried deep inside the playroom chimney so many years before. She thought back to the first time she had seen anyone travel through the chimneys: the shock appearance of Pip, the apprentisweep, flying down her own bedroom chimney and appearing, soot-covered, on her hearth. And her discovery of a secret world of magical chimney sweeps that seemed to reside deep within the walls of the Calendar House itself.

Back then she could never have known that her mother's hidden locket would turn out to be not just a piece of jewellery, but a key: a magical key that allowed ordinary folk to use the ancient sweeps' magick to travel from one chimney to another, reaching almost anywhere in an instant, as long as it had a hearth. This locket was one of the few remaining portals created by the sweeps in times gone by, when magical and ordinary folk mingled together freely and openly, the sweeps keeping and guarding the hearths of all men and women here in Dotty's ordinary world.

And so it was that Dotty was well used to zipping up and down the chimneys; to visit Sylv in Cardiff, mostly (it beat Trans Rail), but also sometimes to travel from room to room within the vast mansion house that since the death of her parents had become her home. My, what a strange and magical home it had turned out to be, Dotty thought.

Nevertheless, chimney travel was still an odd feeling. She closed her eyes for a moment. It wasn't exactly claustrophobic; it was over too quickly to have time to think about being crammed and whizzed through the thousands of tiny tunnels and passages that made up the network of chimneys both within the Calendar

House and beyond. But it was most certainly a strange sensation. It made Dotty's stomach flip, just like one of those swing boat rides at the fairground. Still, she had no time to muse over that now. She took one more deep breath.

"Hold on, Sylv, I'm on my way." Dotty said to herself. And then, without further ado, she stepped straight into the fire.

Chapter 2

Puzzles

*In which Dotty makes a flying visit to Cardiff and Pip
reveals his own puzzling problems*

Dotty stood in the open fire grate. It seemed so
cold and empty. But then she felt the familiar
prick of electricity in the air, and an unseen force
at her heels, picking them up off the floor in the
split second before she took flight. A strange
magical wind whipped around her, tickling her,
tugging at her hair and her clothes, pulling her up
off her feet at a hundred miles an hour. Brightly
coloured sparks of blue and green flew all around
her, lighting up the darkness of the passage of
chimneys as she zipped through them. It gave her
a nervous feeling of excitement, causing
butterflies in her stomach and a strange rush of

elation all at the same time. She would be at Sylv's house in Cardiff in less than a minute.

As Dotty zoomed through the maze of chimneys, her thoughts turned to Joe. How could he have disappeared like that? Could he really have been kidnapped by sweeps? Surely not! After all, Porguss and Poachling were safely in the hands of the Sweeps' Council now.

But if it wasn't them, was there anyone else who could have kidnapped him, and how? Was there another rogue sweep on the loose? No ordinary sweep would have reason to take him, would they?

Dotty considered the alternatives. Perhaps Sylv had got it wrong. It was entirely possible that Joe had just left his bedroom all by himself, leaving his sister Jazz asleep and sneaking out for a walk or whatever small boys did when they left their bedrooms in the middle of the night.

And then what? Had he run into trouble? Dotty didn't like to think about it. It would almost be better if he had been kidnapped by sweeps: whisked off somewhere for some unknowable reason. Oh, she wished she'd stopped and spoken to Pip before she'd left. If rogue sweeps were involved he might have known something about it. But she had been in such a rush to get down to Cardiff. Sylv was in a real state. Still, they could call him when they got there.

There was no more time to think about things as she was arriving at Sylv's now. Her journey started to slow, her movement a sort of controlled falling downwards as she was propelled feet first down the chimney and into her best friend's bedroom. Chimney travel landings were not a very graceful affair. It was pretty much like being dropped out of a first-storey window onto the stone hearth below. Dotty was surprised that more sweeps didn't break an ankle, or at least sprain one, in their daily use of the chimneys. Perhaps sweeps' limbs were more flexible than those of ordinary folk, she mused.

And so it was that Dotty landed, coughing and spluttering from the soot and coal dust, onto the little brown-tiled hearth that served the fireplace in Sylv's tiny bedroom in Cardiff.

Sylv was waiting for her on her bed, facing the fireplace, surrounded by piles of tissues. She had been crying. A lot. On seeing Dotty she jumped up and leapt into Dotty's arms, barely giving her enough time to recover her balance as she landed.

"Oh, Dot! Thank goodness you're here! You've been ages! How many courses *were* there for supper?"

"Sorry, Sylv. I've been as quick as I can, but it took me a while to get out of the kitchen. There was a bit of a kerfuffle with Geoff."

"Well, that comes as no surprise." Sylv rolled red, tearstained eyes.

"Anyway, I'm here now." Dotty was keen to get to the heart of the matter. "Tell me all about Joe. I want to know everything."

Sylv recounted the events of the day before in as much detail as she could, although there wasn't really much to add from the girls' previous conversation. Joe had gone to bed at his usual time. Jazz had been out with her boyfriend, Gavin the butcher's boy, and had come in at around ten. But she hadn't noticed anything unusual.

It was Joe's dad, Mr Raman, who had discovered that Joe was missing. He had gone in to Joe's room the next morning at 5:30 to ask for his help with the morning papers. The police had been called straight away and had crawled over every inch of the place; but no-one could work out how anyone could have broken in to take Joe without disturbing either his parents or his sister in the next-door bedroom. And so they had concluded that either Joe had got up and walked out of the house by himself for reasons unknown, or that the family themselves were somehow responsible.

"I can't tell you how awful it is, Dot. Dad says Mr Raman's a broken man. He's aged ten years overnight. He's even closed the shop."

"You are kidding me," Dotty exclaimed in surprise.

Dotty fell silent. She knew that Joe would never leave the house without letting his parents know where he was going. And as for the idea that Joe's mum and dad were somehow involved in his disappearance, there was just no way. Dotty knew that Joe and his sister had their fallouts, but Dotty was sure that Jazz would never do anything to harm her little brother, even if he did dob her in to their parents on a regular basis about Jazz's exploits with the butcher's boy, Gavin.

"They've had them down the police station and everything, you know," continued Sylv, almost in a whisper now. "It's shocking. They've even questioned Gavin about it. And you can imagine how that's gone down with his dad."

Gavin's dad was the local butcher. He was as big and beefy as one of his prize bulls. Dotty cringed at the thought of his displeasure. Poor Gavin. And poor Jazz.

"So what you're saying," said Dotty "is that if Joe didn't leave his room on his own and his family had nothing to do with it, then the only way he could have left the house is up that chimney. Right?"

"Yes, I suppose."

The two sat in silence once more, Sylv sniffing into her hanky periodically, Dotty thinking. Sylv was right: chimney hopping did seem the only other explanation for what had happened.

"I think we should talk to Pip," said Dotty. "He might know something."

"What? Now? No, Dot, you can't." Sylv looked panicked.

"Don't be daft; he won't mind us calling him. Not in an emergency like this." Dotty stood up from where she had been perched on the bed.

"It's not that it's just that I..."

"What?"

"Oh, nothing," Sylv mumbled.

Dotty strode to the fireplace and rang the little electric servants' bell that sat neatly to the left of the fire surround.

They waited. It was only a few minutes but it seemed like an eternity. Dotty bit her nails whilst Sylv messed with her hair. The sound of voices came from next door, from Dotty's old bedroom. Dotty's house had finally been rebuilt after the fire and a new family had moved in. They had two small children, a boy and a girl much younger than Dotty. She could hear them through the paper-thin walls, laughing and giggling as their mother readied them for bed, and felt a knot of grief in her stomach.

A dog barked in the garden outside. Dotty poked her head out of Sylv's bedroom window to look across at it. It was a mid-sized black-and-white dog of mixed breeding (a Heinz 57, as her dad would have said). It looked friendly enough. For a fleeting moment Dotty felt sad as she remembered her own two dogs, the pugs, Chip and Pin, truffling around in the same back garden when it had been hers, Mam calling them in, fussing over their dirty paws and noses. Her eyes filled with tears. She blinked them back. Where was Pip?

Sylv put an arm round Dotty and gave her shoulder a squeeze. "I know it's hard, Dot."

The girls hugged for a moment. They were interrupted by a small boy tumbling helter-skelter out of the chimney.

"Pip! What took you so long?" Dotty scolded, shaking off her tears.

Pip looked at her crossly, answering her question with a prolonged fit of coughing. "Blasted chimney dust," he muttered.

Sylv's greeting was considerably more welcoming than Dotty's if no less appropriate. She flung herself headlong into the sweep's unsuspecting arms and planted him a big wet kiss on the cheek. "Pip, so good to see you again. It's been too long." Pip gave Sylv his best rakish grin. Sylv blushed.

Tears forgotten, Dotty looked on in horror. Were her two closest friends actually flirting with one another? When had that happened? Clearly she was out of the loop. Surprised to feel herself more than a little irritated at the display of feeling between her two best friends, Dotty did her best to diffuse the situation. "Sylv, put him down," she pouted. "Pip's just fallen out of a chimney, for goodness' sake. With all that hugging, you're making yourself as dirty as he is. Honestly, you might as well go and climb up the chimney and have done with it."

Sylv looked both embarrassed and cross. She took a step back, glaring at her friend, and made a cursory attempt to brush down her now rather grubby onesie.

Pip's cross expression gave way to one of amusement. He gave a low bow. "Greetings, ladies. And what can I do you for this fine evening?" He smiled, his steely blue eyes twinkling out from beneath soot-covered lashes.

Dotty huffed. "There's no time for all that now, Pip. This is serious."

"Well then, you'd better tell me all about it, hadn't you?" He continued to smile sweetly, plonking himself on the corner of the bed. "And sharpish, by the sounds of it."

Keen to do all of the talking in case Sylv decided to make any more of a fool out of herself, Dotty quickly recounted the story of Joe's disappearance. Pip sat quietly throughout, listening intently until she had finished.

"So, Pip, what do you think? It couldn't be Porguss and Poachling, could it?"

"No," he looked puzzled. "The Rogue Sweeps are still safely in the hands of the Council. I know that for a fact. And I don't know of any reason, or of any other sweep who would have cause to take Joe. The only thing I can think of is, well...no it can't be. I just can't see any connection between the two."

"Between the two what? What else has happened?" Dotty asked.

"I don't know," he replied, clearly unsettled. "It's just that there have been some mighty strange goings on lately: things going missing. But they've never taken an actual *person*...And then there's the chimney thefts..."

"What thefts?" asked Sylv. "You mean someone has been stealing chimneys?"

Dotty sniggered at the silly question.

Pip shot Dotty a glance. "Well, in a sort of a way, yes, Miss Sylvia," he said. "That's exactly what has been happening."

Dotty stopped laughing.

Pip continued, "It started off with people's valuables going missing during the night. Small items, mostly: trinkets or jewellery. Anything silver or gold and the odd glass ornament. Thefts any common thief would make. But then things started to get weird. People's chimneys started to disappear."

"But how is that possible?" Dotty asked.

"With faerie magick," replied the boy, "The very same magick you used to escape the rogue sweeps, not so very long ago."

"I don't follow," said Dotty.

Pip let out a small sigh. "You remember how you used a faerie charm to transport your mother's nursery room back to a time when there was an open fireplace in it? Well, just imagine if you used that same magick to wipe out the fireplace altogether; so it was as if there had never been a fire there at all."

Sylv gasped. "Do you think someone could really do that?"

A thousand questions raced through Dotty's mind. Wouldn't they have to have a large supply of faerie charms to achieve such an effect, one for each chimney? And weren't the charms really difficult to get hold of? And would the magick be strong enough to hold? She had thought the magic of a faerie charm was only temporary – not strong enough to remove a fireplace forever. "And anyway why on earth would someone want to do such a weird thing? And what could it possibly have to do with Joe?" she asked, giving voice to her last questions.

Pip answered, "I'm afraid I don't know. We have no records of a sweep ever having done such a thing. There are stories going back deep into ancient lore that speak of faeries being called upon by sweeps to close up a chimney to keep some unnamed evil at bay. But that was hundreds of years ago. To remove a fireplace, depriving sweeps from coming into the world of men for any other reason...well, no sweep would do it. It's a simple as that. A faerie on the other hand, well, who knows what they might do. Tricksy creatures, they are."

Pip adjusted his cloth cap absent-mindedly, looking more perturbed than ever. "As for your friend, Joe, I can't see any obvious link between the two things, so maybe nothing. I mean, there haven't been any reports of people going missing in all this disappearing chimney business."

Dotty sighed. There had to be something they could do. If there was any chance: just the smallest chance she could make a difference. "Well, either way we need to find him, so please can you speak to the Sweep's Council about it?" she asked. "The police are doing nothing and if we suggest he flew out through the chimney they're hardly going to believe us, are they? Even if the Council doesn't know anything perhaps they can send out a search party."

"I'll go straight away," said Pip. "If there is a boy being held captive somewhere, our scouts will find him – don't you worry."

He turned to go.

"Thanks, Pip. We know you'll do what you can," Sylv oozed.

Dotty gave an irritated cough.

Pip formed a small half-smile and then, doffing his cap, bade the girls a hasty goodnight and disappeared back up the chimney.

Puzzles

Chapter 3

Kidnapped

In which Joe finds himself imprisoned and makes a ghastly discovery

Joe woke in the darkness, inhaling sharply at the shock of his surroundings. Where was he? His eyes sprang open but he saw nothing but blackness. He smelled the sweet pungent aroma of straw and felt it underneath him. It poked through the fabric of his thick cotton pyjamas and pricked at his bare feet. Was he in a stable? Joe sat up, drawing his knees up tight to his chest and hugging them. He shivered, as much out of fear as from a lack of warmth. He scanned the room for a sign of his recent captors, but his eyes wouldn't allow him to see anything; not just yet.

Slowly his sight began to adjust to the dimly-lit space. Joe saw now that he wasn't in a stable, but rather that he was in a basement or cellar of sorts. Wherever it was, it was very, very old. Joe knew this instinctively, although he couldn't have said why. Except that it smelled old; it exuded the decaying scent of age and desolation and misery and despair. This was not a happy place. He was scared.

Joe's eyes seemed to be taking a long time to adjust. Was it still dark outside? He couldn't be sure. He could just make out now that the floor was earthen, straw strewn across it as was the custom several hundreds of years ago. He made as if to stand but found himself unable to, bashing his head hard on something above him. He strained his eyes, trying to make out what it was that had assaulted him so harshly. Not quite believing what his eyes were telling him, he reached an arm up over his head, his small hand encircling a thick, cold, iron bar. No! Surely not. It couldn't be! Joe was inside a cage.

He cried out, flinging himself at the bars, taking them in his hands and shaking them, except he already knew that they were far too thick and heavy for someone of his slight frame and size to move. He was quite alone. And quite trapped. Joe slumped back down to the floor. His head hurt.

He could see the room better now. It was actually a lot bigger than he had at first thought.

The dawn was creeping in through a small, dirty pane of glass in a top corner of the room. He peered hopelessly through the bars of his cage. At the far end of the room sat an old scrub-topped table and a solitary chair. There wasn't much on it: just a heavy-looking metal flagon and a wooden plate that held nothing but a few crumbs and a small bone-handled knife. Someone else had been in the room, but whoever they were they weren't here now.

Joe continued to search the cellar, hoping to find a doorway and presumably some stairs, but he couldn't see either. The room simply seemed to have no entrance or exit. He looked up, craning his neck, seeking out evidence of a trap door in the ceiling. Nothing. It just didn't make sense. He surveyed his surroundings one more time.

And then he saw it. He must have missed it the first time because he was intent on finding a doorway. But there it was: a fireplace. It was black and dirty and old, much like the rest of the room. The grate that sat in it was cracked and filthy, spewing out its contents onto the floor; the embers of the fire having long since burnt out.

Joe shuddered as his mind pieced together jumbled fragments of memory from the night before: a dirty, ragged boy; a scuffle; bright flashes of blue and green light. His stomach leapt up into his mouth. And then a man. Joe remembered snatches of gruff, whispered conversation as he had faded in and out of consciousness. But the fireplace; surely he couldn't have come in through the fireplace? He was confused.

As Joe sat staring at the fire, there was a sudden movement in the chimney. He heard a sort of flapping, brushing, scraping sound as something came down the flue. In a moment it appeared, coughing and sneezing as it fought with the cloud of soot and brick dust that descended with it. It was a bird.

The sun was coming up quite quickly now and the room and its contents, although still dimly lit, were altogether clearer. The bird gave itself a shake, settling its tattered grimy feathers, and hopped towards Joe's cage. He recoiled as the bird leaned in towards the bars, its long, sharp beak dangerously close to Joe's small frame; its head cocked on one side in interest.

Boy and bird stared at one another momentarily. Joe saw now that it was a magpie. Its feathers were covered in coal dust so that it was difficult at first to recognise that, its white feathers being themselves almost black with dirt. But no: a magpie it most definitely was.

This was no normal magpie, though. For a start, it was far too big, being the size of a large raven, if not bigger. And then there was the thing that seemed to be strapped over one of its eyes – was it a part of its head, or just attached to it? It looked like some kind of small camera lens, fashioned out of brown leather and metal. Joe watched it buzz and click, making a zipping sound as it focused on him. A small red light flashed on an off and Joe realised in horror that it was an eye: the unholy looking bird had a mechanical eye! Joe fell faint, reeling at the discovery. The bird cocked its head to the other side, whirring and clacking as it refocused its unnatural gaze. Joe now saw that the other eye was clouded and dull – unseeing, where once it would have been bright and enquiring. He felt sick.

"Greetings," croaked the bird.

Kidnapped

Chapter 4

Waiting

In which Dotty tries to find some answers but is presented with only more puzzles

A week had passed since Joe had gone missing and there was still no news, either from the police or the Sweep's Council. Dotty was bursting with frustration at her seeming inability to advance the investigation in some way. She was sure that Joe's disappearance had something to do with the world of the sweeps and she felt that, as one of the few people who knew about them, she should be in a position to help. But other than constantly badger Pip for information, what could she do?

Sitting on her bed doing nothing certainly wasn't the answer. She jumped up and rang the servant's bell in her bedroom impatiently. Well, she didn't ring it, exactly, as there was no longer any 'ring'. But she prodded it, fiercely and repeatedly, in a vain attempt to hasten Pip's arrival. Eventually, he appeared, even more untidy than usual, face dirty, cap lopsided, and looking distinctly unhappy.

"All right, all right, Miss Dotty, keep your 'air on!" he complained, a little less good-naturedly than usual. "You're not the only person ringing my bell, you know."

He wheezed, brushing off his trousers. Dotty noticed that he seemed to be covered in feathers: twigs, and moss sticking to his hair and in his clothes. He bent over to pick a piece of down out from between his blackened, bare toes. "Met with a bird's nest along the way," he explained.

Dotty giggled. It occurred to her that it was the first time she'd really laughed since this whole business with Joe had started.

"So what's all this about, then? What's the hurry?" Pip asked, digging out a twig that had found its way down the back of his shirt. "Was there something you wanted to tell me?"

Dotty's face fell again. "Well, er, no – nothing. I was rather hoping you might have some news for me...about Joe."

"Oh, I see." Pip padded across the hearth rug, settling gently down beside Dotty on her bed. "No, I'm sorry, but the Sweep's Council knows nothing about it. I would have told you if they did." He gave Dotty's hand a gentle squeeze. "Their scouts have carried out an initial search, but weren't able to unearth anything of use. No one seems to have seen or heard anything. Joe seems to have simply vanished into thin air. I'm sorry, Miss Dotty, I was confident we'd find him almost straight away, but I'm afraid we've drawn a blank."

"Well that's just not good enough," she snapped, bursting into tears. She was so frustrated. Poor Joe! Could nobody find him?

Pip put an arm round Dotty, patting her awkwardly on the shoulder. "Now then, miss. Don't fret. If he's out there we'll find him soon enough." He paused for a moment. "But you know, Miss Dotty, you might want to consider: well, you should prepare yourself. What I mean to say is...well, you should think about the possibility that it's nothing to do with us sweeps at all. It may be something best left to your police force."

"No!" Dotty turned, fixing her gaze firmly on him. "It can't be! There's no way he could have got out of that room without the help of sweep's magick! You know it as well as I do..." Dotty trailed off. "I had so hoped he might be being held somewhere, somewhere safe."

"I know, miss, I know." Pip rummaged around inside his waistcoat and produced a remarkably pristine white lace handkerchief from within. He offered it to Dotty.

"Thanks," she sniffed. She sat for a moment, composing herself, and then added, "You know, Joe's sister, Jazz, is always sneaking out to see the butcher's boy. She said she got in at 10.30 that night, but maybe she got in a lot later; or maybe she went out again. Maybe she wasn't there when he went missing at all, which means he could have walked out of the house after all."

Dotty dabbed at her eyes with the handkerchief. It was monogrammed, embroidered in one corner with the letter 'G'. That was her Mam's initial. Dotty looked at Pip in surprise.

"Yes, your mother gave it to me," Pip said. "A long, long time ago. You keep it now." He hopped lightly off the bed. "Now, I have to go. Things to do. And with all these sticks and feathers, I think I might be in need of my annual bath." He grinned. "Bye, Miss Dotty, and chin up," and off he disappeared, back up Dotty's chimney.

Dotty wasted no time Skyping Sylv. After a quick report back to her friend with Pip's findings (or lack of them) in respect of Joe's disappearance, she got straight to the point.

"Sylv, I think we need to speak to Jazz."

"Why? The police questioned her for hours, like."

"Well maybe she didn't tell the truth. Maybe she left the house again, or maybe she never came back. We're assuming sweeps are involved but, in truth, before we can make that assumption we really need to know if he could have left by the door."

"Joe's mam says she checked on them both before she turned in at 11 and that they were both sleeping."

"Yeah, but it was dark, wasn't it? What if she'd put a dummy in the bed so it looked like her? You know: the old pillows under the duvet trick." Dotty smiled grimly. Not that she'd ever tried it herself, but every child knew of that parent-fooling device: well, at least in theory.

"So we should give her a call, right?" Dotty concluded.

"Good luck with that. She's pretty sore about the whole thing, you know. Her mam and dad have stopped her seeing Gavin. She just sits behind the counter in the shop all day now, crying and texting Gavin on her 'phone. She's scaring off all the customers."

Dotty knew it was a long-shot. Jazz was quite a few years older than Dotty and Sylv, very much a teenager, and definitely not interested in anything 'little girls' like them had to say. But she had to try.

Dotty sent her a text. "Hi Jazz, can we talk?" she messaged.

Jazz wasn't online though, and Dotty had to wait four hours until she got a response. It was excruciating.

"Not really in the mood for talking," came back the eventual reply.

"I know. I'm sorry about Joe," wrote Dotty. "I want to help."

"You can't help. Leave it to the police."

"I just wondered if you might have forgotten to tell them something. Or if you were too afraid to."

"Don't you think I'm getting enough grief from my parents about this?" Jazz"s response was angry. "He's my little brother, you know. I love him. I wouldn't lie about sneaking out just to save my own skin. Not if it would find him. You shouldn't have asked, Dotty."

"Jazz, I'm sorry; I'd just hoped the police might have missed something, that's all."

But it was no use. Jazz wouldn't speak to Dotty any more after that.

Dotty felt bad for hurting Jazz's feelings, but she was determined to take something positive away from their talk. If Jazz had definitely been there all the time, it was all the more likely that Joe's disappearance did have something to do with the sweeps after all. So she would just have to keep exploring that avenue instead. Clearly asking Pip about it over and over wasn't getting her anywhere, though. She needed to try something else. Perhaps her uncle would have some answers. After all, he definitely had some sort of connection with the sweeps, even though he had been quick to change the subject whenever she had asked him about it.

There was no time to lose, so Dotty raced straight down the corridor to find him. Upon reaching his study, the door was ajar, but Great Uncle Winchester was not there. "Typical," She grumbled. She stepped inside. The room was in its usual state of utter chaos. Papers covered every available space on floor and walls, its four corners crammed with books and maps and globes and telescopes and model aeroplanes and all manner of other strange and wonderful contraptions. Dotty had no idea what most of them were.

She picked her way over to his desk, it seeming the logical place to start. It was piled high with rolls of thick paper. They appeared to be letters, once sealed with wax, now broken open to read. Dotty picked a few of them up, scanning their contents. The writing was loopy and difficult to read, the ink smudged in places. For the most part, they seemed to Dotty to be records of meetings. There was a lot of talk of the Council, but nothing that interested Dotty or led her any closer to Joe. She still didn't understand why they should be writing to her great uncle about these things either. After all, he wasn't a sweep. She huffed, sitting down heavily on his brown leather office chair.

Crunch. Dotty unearthed yet another squashed roll of parchment from underneath her.

This one had a different colour seal on it – purple, whereas all the others were black. Curious, she unrolled the yellowish paper, scouring it for news of Joe. It seemed the Council had arrested a boy. She read:

> *"The disgraced apprentisweep, Skitter, on initial questioning has revealed his connection to a gang that he claims is responsible for the recent widespread disappearance of chimneys. We believe that further discussion with the boy may lead to his disclosure of the whereabouts of the gang or its leader. A meeting has been convened..."*

A meeting! At last something was happening. Perhaps it would bring news of Joe. Before she could read on, a set of spidery fingers seemed to reach from out of nowhere. They snatched the paper from over Dotty's shoulder, crumpling it, preventing her from reading any more.

Dotty shrieked. "Hey, I was reading that," she spun around to discover the owner of the hand. It was Strake.

"Tut, tut, Miss Parsons. What would Mr Winchester have to say about this, I wonder?"

"I wasn't doing anything wrong," argued Dotty.

"We shall see," was the response. "For now I should be grateful if you would leave his office." Strake waved her airily towards the door with one spindly arm. "And you needn't think about returning," he added. "I shall be keeping an eye on things here until he returns."

"And when will that be?" asked Dotty.

"I really couldn't say," he smiled at her, silkily.

Horrid man, she thought.

Her discovery had left Dotty feeling more frustrated than ever. Now she knew there was a meeting, but she didn't know where or when, and she couldn't ask Great Uncle Winchester about it because he had gone and disappeared again. She couldn't go back to the office because Strake would be guarding it, now he knew there was something of interest in there.

That left as her only course of action for the minute, Pip, although he was already pretty fed up with her calling him all the time. She decided to call him anyway, but he wasn't answering, no matter how many times she pressed the servant's bell. She was beginning to get really cross. She really didn't know what else she could do.

The next twenty-four hours seemed an eternity. To Dotty it seemed that a cloud had descended over the Calendar House and, no matter what they did, the house's few residents seemed unable to shift it. Dotty just didn't feel like exploring the garden with Geoff, a pastime she usually loved; and she couldn't concentrate enough to read a book in the library, her mind constantly wondering off to thoughts of Joe and the mystery meeting. Even spending time in Mam's playroom for the first time seemed pointless.

Gobby did her best to cheer Dotty up, cooking up a storm and making all Dotty's favourite treats and cakes, but she seemed to have lost her appetite. In the end she took to staring out of her bedroom window, waiting impatiently for Pip or her uncle to resurface, and wondering where Joe could have got to, praying for his safety.

At last, as night fell, Dotty managed to find some solace staring out of her bedroom window, across to the vastness of the lake. She found its cool, dark waters somehow intoxicating, mesmerising. There was something odd, though. There seemed to be lights out on the water. She had walked with Geoff down to the lake many times before, going all around it on some of their longer walks, and so she knew that there were no manmade lights down there: no lanterns, no lamps marking the path, no lights strung across the boat house. Nothing.

So just where were the lights coming from, exactly? Dotty wondered if it might be the gardener, Kenny, doing a spot of night fishing, or patrolling the grounds. But if there was a person wandering about with a torch it would have been obvious. And besides, she would have seen him. No, these lights were something else.

Dotty pondered the strange lights. Whatever could they be? And what was their source? She wondered if the explanation could be a magical one. After all, if there were magical chimney sweeps, surely there must be other magical beings, too. Pip had already told her about faeries. Perhaps that was what they were? Or will 'o the wisps maybe? Or sprites, or elves or, well—who knew?

The more she looked at them, however, the more Dotty realized that they appeared to be shining from *under* the lake. Of course, if she was going with the 'magical beings' theory, it could be water nymphs, perhaps. But then it could just as easily be some previously-undiscovered species of freshwater fish: ones that glowed like the deep water jellyfish she had seen on TV.

It frustrated Dotty not knowing what they were, and it annoyed her that she felt she was going to have to ask Pip about it. Like pretty much everything else around here, she thought resentfully. Of course, she could find out for herself. She could take Geoff down to the water and find out first-hand what they were. But quite frankly, even with the dog for company, the thought of doing that when it was so dark outside was just a little too scary to contemplate.

So, feeling as if she were sinking under the weight of yet another unanswered question, she resigned herself for now to simply staring at the unfathomable lights and pondering hopelessly at their meaning.

Chapter 5

Lights on the Lake

In which Dotty discovers the true nature of the strange lights on the water

It was early morning and there was still no sign of either Great Uncle Winchester or Joe. Feeling a little braver with the dawn, Dotty decided to take the dog for a walk down by the lake. What those strange lights were was one question she might be able to find an answer to by herself, at least. She wasn't holding out too much hope, now that it was daytime, though.

The weather remained cold, as if refusing to recognise the onset of spring, turning the dew into frost on the ground. Dotty trudged with Geoff through the still-slumbering garden, her breath visible in the cold, crisp air. Kenny had warned her to keep off the paths, as the ice made them treacherous, so she walked along the grass instead. The frost-covered verges gave a satisfying crunch underfoot, leaving bright green, watery footprints in the grey blanket that covered them. Geoff seemed happy enough, snuffling in amongst the skeletons of the bare bushes, seeking out a snail, or the remnant of a bone, or the smell of a cat that had long since fled. Dotty wondered how his paws did not freeze, coming into contact again and again with the cold, icy ground, and shivered at the thought.

She glanced down at the lake beyond and noticed that it had frozen over. She had to confess, to herself at least, that she was a little scared of the lake now. Not knowing the source of the strange lights that had illuminated it the previous night made her nervous of what, or who, they might be. Were they friend or foe? As she neared it, she shivered. She wished she had worn her gloves.

But the vast lake, when she reached it, seemed determined to keep its secrets also. A layer of ice covered it, rendering it silent and still. She stared at it. There were no lights. Perhaps the lights had stopped because it was frozen. Maybe whatever caused the lights was frozen, too. Or maybe they had simply stopped because it was daylight. It was no use, for today at least, the lake wasn't giving up its secrets. She would simply have to ask Pip next time she saw him. Not that there was any guarantee that he would know, of course. After all, he didn't know everything: he didn't know about Joe.

Dotty wondered about the meeting of the Sweeps' Council; if only she had been able to find out when it was. If this boy the letter had spoken of could lead the Sweep's Council to the gang of thieves or, even better, their leader, they might also uncover the mystery behind the disappearing chimneys. That would surely be a relief to the Council as, if Pip's reports were true, they were vanishing at quite an alarming rate. But more importantly, oh so much more importantly, it might lead to news of Joe. She was sure the two things were somehow connected. She could feel it.

Dotty had to wait the whole of the next day before she saw Pip again, but finally that night he decided to make her a house call. She was sitting in her usual spot, curled up on the window seat in her bedroom, staring out over the lake, arms hugging her knees. It was eight o'clock. The lights had started glowing eerily again on the water, twinkling and glowing despite the chill, and looking altogether like hazy fireflies on a midsummer's eve.

Pip, somewhat miraculously, managed to make his entrance without his usual fit of coughing and flapping and landed almost daintily on the fireside rug with barely a stumble. As such, Dotty was unaware of his presence on her hearth and jumped almost out of her skin when he tapped her on the shoulder and addressed her with his customary, "Evening, Miss."

But it was not Pip's stealthy approach that was the biggest surprise in store for Dotty. More of a shock was the sight that met her when she turned around to greet him. At first Dotty didn't recognise the boy who stood behind her and greeted her in such a familiar way. Pip was clean!

How handsome he was underneath all that ash and coal dust. His bright blue eyes twinkled from under a smart, tweed cloth cap. His white shirt sleeves billowed out of his buttoned waistcoat, a little sooty from his journey (he had just travelled down a chimney, after all), but for the most part unsoiled. His outfit was completed with freshly-laundered britches, woollen stockings and – shoes! Pip was wearing a pair of hobnailed boots. Dotty had never seen Pip in shoes before; or socks, for that matter.

But the most startling and obvious transformation was his hair. Pip had the most beautiful blond hair. Dotty was so used to seeing Pip covered in dirt and grime she had almost forgotten that his hair was blond, the only reminder of this usually being a circle of marginally-cleaner hair that he hid underneath his cap.

Pip removed his cap and Dotty caught her breath. His entire head seemed to shine and sparkle golden in the lamplight. Dotty uttered an involuntary 'Wow'.

Pip gave his most dazzling white smile, making Dotty flush. Desperate for Pip not to see how impressed she was at his transformation, she found her tongue and quickly thought up the most flippant remark she could muster, which was, "When you said you were having your annual bath, I didn't think you actually *meant* it."

"Bathed and laundered, Miss. I'm glad you're impressed." He grinned.

"Not impressed, just surprised is all," Dotty retorted. "Gave them to your mother to wash, did you?"

"I have no mother, Miss Dotty. I did it all by myself," he replied.

Suddenly Dotty wondered about Pip's family. She had never really considered it before, always having been too tied up in her own crises to stop and think. But now she had more time to reflect, and there were clearly some questions to be answered. Pip had said that he had no mother, but did he have a family...of any sort? Did Sweeps have families?

And, more to the point, how *old* was Pip? He looked like a slightly smaller than average 13-year-old boy, but he said he had known Dotty's mother. He had even given Dotty one of her mother's handkerchiefs last time he had seen her. He might have found it, she supposed, but what would be the point of saying her mother had given it to him if it wasn't the case? No, it must be true.

And if that was true, well that could mean only one of two things: either her mother had visited the Calendar House in the last ten years or so without Dotty's knowledge, or Pip was a *lot* older than he looked. Whichever it was, something definitely didn't add up. Dotty mentally added it to her list of unanswered questions about the strange goings on in her new home.

Pip coughed politely, guiding her attention back to his newly-washed form. "I'm guessing you might like an update on the Council's findings, Miss?"

"Yes, of course. Tell me: have you news on Joe?"

"Well, no," he replied, "but there is something else. It seems we've made a breakthrough, Miss Dotty: about the thefts, that is."

Straight away, Dotty thought of the letter.

"The Sweep's Council has captured a boy named Skitter," Pip continued. "A bad lot: well known by us sweeps. He was picked up for questioning by the Council after making an illegal chimney hop to the outside world."

"That's what I was going to tell you, too," said Dotty. "There was a letter about it in Great Uncle Winchester's study. What's an illegal chimney hop?"

Pip looked surprised. "It's just going somewhere you're not allowed to go, basically. For Skitter, it's travelling anywhere outside the world of sweeps. He's a well-known thief and so the Council banned him. Anyway, that's not the important thing. It seems the Council struck lucky."

"Mm, hmm," Dotty had started to stare out of the window again. Those lights were mesmerising.

Pip carried on, "it seems the boy has managed to get himself involved with a gang of thieves and he says he will tell us not only their whereabouts but the name of their leader, in exchange for his freedom. Turns out he has a little sister he's keen to get back to. No other family, you see. Anyway, there is to be a hearing tonight in the Great Chamber of the Sweep's Council to question him officially. Miss Dotty, are you listening?"

Dotty wasn't. She knew how important this meeting might be but, try as she might, she just couldn't concentrate. The lights on the water were just too distracting. She stared at them. They gave the lake a halo-like glow. Their other-worldly presence bothered her; frightened her.

"Sorry, Pip. So when's the meeting?" she asked.

Pip looked exasperated. "What exactly is it you're staring at, Miss Dotty?"

"It's the lights: the lights on the lake."

"Oh, don't worry about those; they are just the lights from the Grand Chamber. They shine up through the lake when the Council is meeting."

"I don't understand," said Dotty. "That can't be. There isn't a building there."

"Oh but there is, Miss. Under the water. There's really nothing to be afraid of. I promise. Here, why don't I show you?"

"What? You mean go outside?" Dotty balked. "With you? To the lake? Now? No way!"

Pip laughed, "Seriously, Miss. There's nothing scary about it. Cross my heart. Come on – it's a lovely clear night: perfect for skating. Look, I even have my boots on," he said, pointing to his freshly-covered feet. "Go on, I dare you."

Unable to resist the challenge, Dotty conceded. Besides, she had been dying to see the lights up close since yesterday. "Okay, let me find a coat."

As the pair walked down towards the lake, the twilight turned into a beautiful clear night. The stars twinkled in a blanket of rich, blue velvet sky and the moon shone silver over the ground. It occurred to Dotty that she had never been outdoors with Pip before, and that it felt rather strange, seeing this newly clean version of him walking beside her, just like any ordinary boy might do. It almost had a date-like quality about it, Dotty thought, and then quickly dismissed the idea from her mind.

Pip put her arm through his as they walked, giving it a bit of a squeeze. She felt a shiver. Were they really walking arm in arm, she and Pip? She couldn't wait to tell Sylv. Oh gosh, but then Sylv really liked him too. That was obvious from the last time they saw each other. Dotty saw a big problem looming. She wasn't going to give up this moment, though, not for anything. For now, that problem could wait.

"You're shivering," said Pip. "A bit of skating will soon warm you up," he reassured her.

Dotty's focus shifted to the lake. There was a definite eerie light emanating from it, yellow like the glow of lamplight. It was unnatural – creepy even. Dotty hesitated, not wishing to get any closer.

"It's all right, miss. You see, there really is no need to fret. It's just the lights from the ballroom under the lake shining up through the water." He tugged her hand.

"Please, call me Dotty,"

"Okay miss. Dotty, I mean," he said, smiling in the glow of the lamplight as it shone up from the depths below.

On reaching the water's edge they stopped, Pip testing the strength of the ice with his boot for a moment, before sliding out onto the ice. "It's the perfect night for it," he said, grinning rakishly.

Dotty watched with uncertainty as Pip did a quick circuit of the near side of the lake. His form looked graceful and fluid on the frozen water; his movement effortless, weightless almost. The lights shone out from beneath him, so that his form made no shadow on the ice. Then, returning to where she was standing, he did a fancy turn and stood with his hand outstretched, calling her. "Come on. It's quite safe, I promise."

"Show off," Dotty teased, stalling a little. Whilst her roller blades were almost like a second pair of feet to her, she had never been ice skating before. There was a plastic skating rink back home in Cardiff. Sylv had been once, but Dotty had never been herself as her mam hated skating.

"It's okay, Dotty. I'll hold you up. You won't fall – trust me," Pip gave her his most reassuring smile. "And besides," he winked, "you're as sure-footed as a goat."

Dotty looked again at the frozen water, the glow obscuring that which lay beneath. Gingerly she stepped out onto the ice and towards Pip's beckoning form. Almost at once her legs went out from under her, feet flying in all directions. She let out a small shriek of alarm but Pip had her safely in his grasp, saving her from sitting down heavily on the cold, wet ice.

Before Dotty was able to complain, Pip swept her upright, picking her up with a grip that hinted at a strength not suggested by his slight frame. Taking her left hand in his, the other quickly and deftly encircled Dotty's waist, both guiding and supporting her as he ushered her away from the edge of the lake. Dotty tensed, her face feeling hot, despite the cold. But then she relaxed a little and let Pip take the lead as her escort. Before very long she was moving quite naturally on the ice, her legs no longer skating away from under her as Pip chatted away merrily, all the while distracting her from the frozen depths below. As she gazed at him, for the briefest moment, she almost forgot her lost friend.

"So tell me about the lights again, Pip – this ballroom under the lake. Do the sweeps have parties there?" Dotty glanced downwards to inspect the ethereal yellow glow emanating from the water below.

"No, it was never a sweep's ballroom. But it used to be used for very lavish parties in its day." Pip spun Dotty around on the ice. "It was actually first made for the Winchester family: the builders of the Calendar House. It was a folly of sorts – built to show off their wealth and power. The reeds floating in the lake above its glass roof makes it look like a huge mass of stained glass. It's amazing."

"Oh," said Dotty. "Under a lake still seems a bit of a strange place to put a ballroom to me."

"Maybe," agreed Pip. "But it's still pretty cool. Anyway, there came a time when they had no more time or need for parties, so we came to use it instead."

"And how do you get to it?" Dotty asked.

"Well us sweeps come in through the chimney, of course."

"There's a chimney in the ballroom?"

"Obviously," replied Pip impatiently. "You can see it, actually. The top of the chimney comes out in the middle of the lake. It looks like a disused fountain, but if you look closely, you can tell."

"Ooh! Let me see," begged Dotty. Pip guided her over towards the centre of the lake so she could have a look. Sure enough, there was an elaborately carved chimney quite clearly poking out in the middle. From the shore she had always just assumed it was a stone statue.

"The Winchesters built an underground tunnel that led directly from under the house all the way down here to the lake for their own use." Pip added. "The entrance to it's a closely-guarded secret, of course."

"Wow!" Dotty wondered where it could be. She would have to ask Great Uncle Winchester about it, or maybe Gobby; she knew every inch of the house inside out.

"So, Pip, if it's not used for parties, what do the sweeps use it for?"

"As I said before, it's now the grand meeting chamber for the Council of Sweeps. They do all their official business there:

important Council meetings, the annual national Sweep's convention, Sweep trials..."

"You mean, like a court house?"

"Precisely. That's where the dreaded sweep traders were brought to account by the Council and ordered to be imprisoned for their attempts to steal the Calendar House Key."

Dotty shuddered at Pip's reference to the evil rogue sweeps, Porguss and Poachling. They might have lost the fight to take the key but, nevertheless, she didn't want to have to tangle with them again in a hurry. She grasped the locket around her neck protectively and glanced down at the water, unable to escape the fleeting image in her mind of one of their greasy, chubby hands rising up through the water to grab it. Dotty suddenly hoped the ice was very, very thick.

"And we might have the odd *one or two* parties..."

Dotty spent the next ten minutes trying to wheedle out of Pip when there might be such a party and whether she might be allowed to attend. She had never seen a big gathering of sweeps all together and it intrigued her – almost as much as the idea of a ball, given that she'd never been to one of those, either, with or without sweeps. But Pip remained smugly tight-lipped on the subject, and in the end she let it go.

Presently, their conversation returned to the Council. "Of course, if I'd had *my* way," Pip resumed, "I would have seen your Mister Strake before the Council, too. But of course Mr Winchester wouldn't hear of it."

Dotty had never understood her great-uncle's insistence on protecting his personal secretary, when Strake had so blatantly abused his trust, plotting against him with Porguss and Poachling—not to mention threatening Dotty and her friends. What *was* the bond that held them together so closely, in spite of Strake's betrayal? There was so much she still didn't understand. She was determined to find out the answer to all her questions though. But for now, she needed to answer the most pressing question: where was Joe?

Pip continued, "...and, of course, there's the questioning of the thief coming up this very night. That'll be interesting, I should wager. Oh what I'd give to be there and hear that miserable wretch explain himself in front of the Sweeps' Council."

"Tonight?" Dotty asked.

"Yes, I already said that," scolded Pip. "Weren't you listening to a word I was saying to you earlier?"

"Er, well, yes I was - sort of," Dotty looked sheepish. "But if it's tonight, we need to get in."

"We can't. I'm too junior to be allowed, being only an apprentisweep."

"Surely you can sneak us in, Pip? If it's as big a room as you say, no-one would notice."

"Yes, believe me, they would. And if I got caught they'd take away my apprenticeship."

"But there might be news of Joe."

"I know. I'm sorry, Dotty but I just can't risk it." He stopped on the ice, facing her. "You understand?"

"Not really," she pouted.

"Come on," Pip said, taking Dotty's hand. "It's late. We'd better get back."

Annoying as it was, it seemed they had no choice but to have to wait another day.

"So tell me about this gang again," Dotty asked as they walked back up the terracing that rose up towards the house. "Do they know anything about it yet, or why they're stealing the chimneys?"

"No," said Pip. "Hopefully they'll find out tonight. The only thing he's given us so far is the name of their leader. Apparently he goes by the name of the Vagabond King."

Chapter 6

Conversation

In which Joe hears news of a visitor

Joe sat in his darkened room. It surprised him how quickly his situation had become normal to him. He no longer awoke shocked to find himself imprisoned in a dirty cage in some unknown underground location; rather he came to in a state of accepting misery: unhappy and alone, but nevertheless unsurprised.

To say Joe was alone wasn't entirely true, of course; there was the bird. *That* bird: his gaoler. Joe's incarceration was one thing, but having a bird as a prison keeper - now that really wasn't something he could get used to, despite the magpie's all-too-regular presence. Morning and night (insofar as Joe could tell from the limited light in the room) it flapped in noisily through the great open fireplace, coughing and spluttering, shedding its dirty, untidy feathers about the place, and clicking and whirring as it focused its awful mechanical eye on Joe to croak a greeting.

The bird's twice-daily visits brought with them food and an unpleasant company of sorts, as it poked its food offering through the bars of Joe's cage with its razor-sharp beak. The meagre meals, habitually wrapped in a dirty cloth, usually comprised a hunk of stale black bread and a piece of dry cheese. Under the watchful mechanical eye of his captor, Joe ate them hungrily, for there was no other source of food.

Occasionally the magpie would speak to Joe. This was actually less unsettling than its mechanical eye which, in his opinion, was downright creepy. As for the speech, Joe was a bright boy and he knew that magpies, crows, and ravens could all be taught to speak, just like parrots or even his pet budgerigar, Eric. Joe missed Eric. He hoped his sister was looking after him properly – giving him the treats that he liked, making sure his cage was clean (unlike Joe's).

Now Joe knew how Eric felt, being cooped up in a cage for most of the day, and understood why he got so excited, flapping his little wings and darting excitedly about the room, when Joe's mam let him release the bird into their small upstairs sitting room above the shop. He thought he might let Eric go when he got out of here. *If* he got out of here...

Joe wished that he could stand up in the cage. His legs felt cramped: unused, wasted. Joe was a studious boy; and whilst it was true to say that he had always been happier with his books and his learning than playing football in the park, now all he longed for was to run around, and jump and play with the other children on Wyvern Road. He could think of nothing more perfect at this moment than to kick a ball around with Billy Evans from number 5, or to play a game of tag with Sylv and, most of all, Dotty. He missed Dotty. She had been Joe's favourite before she had moved away from the street. She was always the best at tag.

This morning the bird seemed rather more perky than usual. It hopped awkwardly around the cellar, inspecting the corners with its beak, picking up stray pieces of straw and sweeping the crumbs from the dirt floor with a tattered wing. It was clearly attempting to tidy the room, although as fast as the bird tidied, its ill-fitting feathers shed on the ground, only serving to make the space ever more unkempt. Joe, who was inquisitive by nature, watched the display with some interest. Finally, unable to contain himself any longer, he plucked up the courage to speak to the bird and find out what it was up to.

He ventured a cough, trying to get the bird's attention. The bird ignored him, continuing at its futile business, its eye buzzing and clicking as it went. Joe tried again. "Erm, Mr Bird – what are you doing? Are you tidying? Is someone coming to see us?"

The bird turned sharply, the eye whizzing into focus, the tiny red light shining fully into Joe's eyes. Joe blinked rapidly, momentarily blinded.

"The King," the magpie rasped; its gravelly voice like the crackle of broken glass underfoot. "We be expecting a visit from the King."

And in the next moment, whilst Joe was still rubbing his eyes and trying to rid himself of the red spots of light that still danced before them, the bird was gone.

Alone once more, Joe wondered who the important visitor that the bird had talked about could be. Were they a real person, this king? And should their coming be feared or welcomed? Could it be the king of the magpies? He certainly hoped not; that was just too creepy for words. And in any case Joe couldn't imagine that there was more than one of those awful, unnatural creatures. But if not a bird, who then?

Oddly enough, at the mention of the king, Joe couldn't help but think of his dad. Eddie Raman was a huge Elvis Presley fan and always referred to the singer as 'the King'. On this basis Joe half-expected that, when the visitor finally did arrive, he would be a large middle-aged man, sporting huge sideburns and a spangly cat suit. Joe formed a half-smile: the first unterrified thought that had entered his mind since his capture. Unfortunately for Joe, the image he had formed in his mind couldn't have been further from the reality of what was to come.

Conversation

Chapter 7

Questioning Skitter

In which the Council attempts to learn more about the Vagabond King

The broom struck the marble floor of the cavernous hall three times. *'Crack, crack, crack'*, the sound echoed around the room, calling the assembly to be silent. A hush fell over the grand ballroom under the lake.

"Bring in the boy," the Council Master ordered.

There was a scraping and a shuffling as a small boy was brought forwards in shackles attended by two burly sweeps in official-looking uniforms, rows of mother of pearl buttons twinkling against the black of their suits. The prisoner made a pitiful sight. Pale, thin and meagre, his clothes were so threadbare that they seemed to be held together by nothing but the dirt that covered them. The boy's bare blackened feet were bird-like in their emaciated condition, his knees swollen and calloused from being forced up chimneys without the help of sweeps' magick. His eyes darted wildly from side to side, like an animal ensnared and looking for escape. He looked around, eyes and nose watering, breathing shallow. The boy picked absent-mindedly at a sore on his hand. Every muscle in the prisoner's body looked tense, as if ready for flight, given the very slightest of opportunities. Were it not for this, the burly escorts looked entirely unnecessary for such a scrap of a boy.

There was an echo of hushed conversation amongst the assembly. The Council Master quieted them with another tap of his broom. Then, at length, he spoke. "What is your name, boy?"

"They call me Skitter," his voice was barely above a whisper.

"Are you the Skitter known to the Council for breaking your bonds of apprenticeship these three years since on grounds of stealing from the homes of the chimneys you swept; for which crime you were removed from the position of apprentisweep and banned from ever again carrying the name of Sweep?"

"Yes," replied the boy, miserably. "But I had to. My..."

"And are you the same Skitter who has been brought before the Council these nineteen times since on counts of vagrancy and petty thievery?" cut in the Council Master.

"I am," the boy pleaded, "but..."

"And were you three nights hence caught in an illegal chimney hop into the world of the Ordinary Folk, an undertaking strictly forbidden to you by this very Council?" the Council Master thundered.

"Yes," conceded the boy, utterly wretched.

"It seems to me, Master Skitter, that you are a thorn in the side of the Sweeps Council. A thorn is a dangerous thing. Whilst a single prick can seem of little consequence, a continued pricking from that same thorn, or a number of thorns, can soon lead to an altogether more serious injury: one which is less easy to heal. Such wounds can become infected, Master Skitter. And I fear that you bear the source of that infection.

"It is my personal opinion that if more stringent action is not taken against you now, that you will continue to inflict injury upon us. However, the Council is divided. I understand you have agreed to disclose your actions, fully and frankly, and to reveal the identity of those for whom you work, in exchange for which the Council will be lenient. In short, boy, you have been given an opportunity to explain yourself."

A silence came over the room, punctuated only by the whimpering of the boy, whether through fear or self-pity it was impossible to tell.

"We are waiting," the Council Master prompted the sorry wretch.

"I did it for the King," the boy answered simply, his voice barely audible in the vast auditorium.

"Speak up. The Council must hear you."

"The King: I was on a matter of business for the King!" he repeated. His voice was louder this time; more firm, as if saying the name gave him a confidence of sorts. A murmur ran across the room.

"And who is this King?" questioned the Council Master. "This person of whom you speak: is this the name you give to your new master, the leader of your band of thieves?"

"Ha!" cried the boy, suddenly animated. "The King is far more than a master to me. He is a friend, a comrade, a father. He is the greatest sweep that ever walked these blessed streets, and your pointless little Council is nothing compared to him." He spat. A maniacal light danced in his eyes. No longer cowering, he drew himself up to his full height and surveyed the room meeting anyone who met his gaze with gleeful defiance.

"Oh yes," he continued. "The King has a plan all right. And it will bring an end to your Council and its insistence on meddling in the lives of the ordinary folk; an ignorant race so blind to the world around them that even in the darkness of the chimneys we see so much more clearly than they will ever do. Never was a race less deserving of our loyalty and protection. They have no magick, no knowledge. And yet we guard them like faithful dogs. Well, no more! My master sends me here to you with a message: the Sweeps will be servants no longer! The King has arrived and, once his plans are complete, we will be free of this world of ordinary folk – forever!"

A clamour broke out across the grand ballroom; hundreds of angry faces shouted their dissent at the lone boy in the centre of the room. The Council Master struck his broom against the stone floor again and again, fighting to regain the order of the house.

The boy laughed; a mad, sickening laugh, a high-pitched chattering that rose to the top of the auditorium and reverberated off the glass. Threats rang out across the room. The Council Master banged his broom once more, calling for silence, but the crowd was out of control.

"The boy is mad," they cried

"A lunatic!"

"There is no King but in his own sorry head."

"Oh, but there is a King," the prisoner spoke to his audience. "And he is every bit as real as any of you who stand in this chamber."

The crowd erupted again.

"Mark my words," he shrieked above the din. "The King *is* coming. You will never catch him, but you will all learn to know him and to fear him. By the time he has finished with you, the only name on the lips of this Council will be that of the Vagabond King!"

The crowd roared, out of control, the boy madly gleeful at the descent into chaos.

"Take him down," the Council Master gave the instruction to the guards. Struggling against his bonds, the boy was manhandled out of the room and into the depths below.

Chapter 8

Stops and Starts

In which Dotty has a spat with Pip and speaks to Great Uncle Winchester

Long after Pip had left her, Dotty sat at her bedroom window watching the lights on the lake. They did seem particularly bright tonight, setting the whole lake aglow with their yellowish aura. But perhaps that was because she now knew what the lights signified. That there, even at that very moment, deep under the lake, and beneath the exact spot where she and Pip had skated, was a meeting of the Council of Sweeps: a very important meeting upon which the whole future of her friend, Joe, might rest.

She wondered what the outcome might be, and whether the Council might come any closer to finding Joe. The police were certainly no further forward with their search. It seemed as if they had given up already, consigning Joe's file to a pile of runaways a mile deep. Poor, poor Joe: he must be so lost and alone right now.

Only when, one by one, the lights went out, plunging the lake into silent darkness, did she take herself wearily to bed. Climbing in heavy-limbed, she let a troubled sleep overtake her, both hopeful and fearful in equal measure as she drifted off. She dearly wished that the boy that Pip had spoken of, this sweep-thief, would be able to tell them where her missing friend was, if he knew. But it was late now. Whatever news there was, whether good or bad, Pip would bring it in the morning. For now, all Dotty could do was hope.

The sun was only just coming up when Dotty was awakened by Pip arriving on her hearth. But it was not with the good report she had longed for. Looking much more like his usual filthy self (albeit that his hair was still distinctly cleaner than it had been before his annual bath), Pip broke the news.

"Things are far worse than we imagined. By the sounds of it, this Vagabond King and his band are much larger, and their plan more carefully thought out, than the Council had thought possible. It seems he wants to separate the world of the sweeps from that of the ordinary folk forever, and he's losing no time in going about it." He sighed.

"The sweeps are already struggling to go about their business. Their paths of travel are so restricted with all the chimney disappearances. And of course, once there are no more chimneys to look after, they will simply have no business in the world of Men."

"But what about Joe?" pressed Dotty, impatiently. "You said they were going to find out about him."

"I know. We truly had hoped the boy would give up some information on his whereabouts, but he wouldn't tell us anything. His loyalty to the Vagabond King is surprisingly fierce."

"But, from what you're saying, we still don't even know if the Vagabond King has Joe, or if a link exists between his disappearance and the plans of this mad man. As far as we know, Joe might well have run away – just like the police said," she concluded. But she knew in her heart of hearts this wasn't true. Joe just wasn't that sort of boy and, even though there seemed nothing to connect them, she couldn't believe that the recent troubles of the sweeps and her friend's simultaneous disappearance were simply a coincidence.

"So just how are we going to find Joe?" Dotty pressed. "Clearly the Council needs to question Skitter again. Even if it's to confirm that he doesn't know anything."

"I'm sure they will, but that is out of our hands," Pip replied. "I simply don't have the clout to go making demands like that of the Council. As I said to Miss Sylvia, perhaps if we were to speak to..."

"You've spoken to Sylv about this?" Dotty exclaimed. "But when?"

"Last night, after the council meeting. You were..."

"Unbelievable!" Dotty exploded. "And since when was Sylv your best friend or you hers? I can't believe you went to see her first. After last night; and when you could have come to see me."

"I did try to, Dotty, but you was..."

"I don't care what you *was*," Dotty retorted. "Just get out. Go and speak to your girlfriend! If you don't have any news on Joe you're no use to me anyway."

"But Miss, you was..."

"Get out!" shrieked Dotty.

"...asleep" muttered Pip resignedly under his breath, and hopped back up the chimney.

Dotty was angry, alone, desperate. She didn't know what to do or where to turn. And now on top of everything else she now felt that even her two best friends were against her. She saw no way of finding Joe and neither the sweeps nor the police seemed to be in any position to help. She felt so desperately that she must act: find Joe, before something dreadful happened to him, if it hadn't already. But what could she do that so many others could not?

Feeling completely at a loss and more than a little betrayed, Dotty slouched down to the kitchen for something to eat. Although in truth she wasn't quite sure whether the knot in her stomach was the symptom of hunger or worry. As she opened the door of the back stairs and stepped down into the kitchen she was greeted by Gobby. The cook bore her usual cheery demeanour. That, at least, could be relied upon, except for those occasions when Geoff was in the room.

"Ah, there you are, Dotty. I was just going to call you for—but why so glum?" Gobby's expression clouded over. "Come now, child. Take a seat by the fire with me and tell old Mrs Gobbins all about it." She ushered Dotty into an easy chair that sat by one of four cast iron ranges that dominated the kitchen of the vast house. The old cook fussed and clucked around her in a motherly way, plumping the cushions on the chair and pulling across a low stool to settle herself by Dotty's side.

At this, the tears began to roll down Dotty's face, the cook's kindness washing away the last of her resolve not to cry. "Oh, Mrs Gobbins, I just can't bear it! Joe going missing, and all that worry: his poor family. And now Sylv being all pally with..." Dotty stopped herself just in time from mentioning Pip. She still wasn't sure whether

Gobby knew about Pip or the sweeps. She sobbed openly instead.

"So you've had a spat with your friend, Sylvia, have you?" Gobby went straight to the heart of the matter. "Well, don't you worry your head about that, child. Take it from an old woman who knows: true friends don't quarrel for long. It'll all be forgotten before you know it." She nodded to herself sagely.

"And as for the terrible business with that poor little boy, Joe, why don't you speak to your great-uncle about it? I'm surprised you haven't talked with him about it before now, actually. He has a nose for these things, Heaven alone knows. But just try him dear. He might well surprise you."

"I've tried," complained Dotty. "But he's never here." He was always so busy and so often away, or holed up in his study doing some important work or other.

"Well he is there now; I know that for a fact. I've just taken his breakfast order." The cook dusted down her apron, matter-of-factly.

Of course Gobby was right, thought Dotty, gathering momentum as she considered the idea. He was certainly in the know – the letter she had read in his study proved that. Not only did her great-uncle have the advantage of knowing about the sweeps, unlike Gobby; clearly he also had some sort of authority over the Council.

She made up her mind. "Thank you, Mrs Gobbins. I'll do that straight away." Dotty stood up and made for the door.

Gobby stopped Dotty with an impromptu hug. "Just don't you fret, child. It'll all turn out all right in the end – you'll see if I'm not right." She wiped Dotty's tear-stained cheeks with a corner of her apron, smearing Dotty with flour.

"Now, if you're going in to see your uncle you can save my poor legs and take him his breakfast whilst you're at it." She pointed to a tray laden down with a full teapot, an enormous stack of blueberry pancakes, a bowl of whipped cream, and a generous jug of warm syrup.

"Here, you can use the trolley. It'll save you spilling. Mr Strake can collect it later on when he returns for Mr Winchester's lunch."

The cook busied herself making the tray ready, adding a bowl of strawberries and a dish filled with bacon that she took from a waiting oven. Dotty grimaced at the mention of Strake. But, feeling distinctly encouraged by Gobby's pep talk, she trotted off, wheeling the breakfast cart in front of her, the stack of pancakes wobbling precariously and threatening to topple as she went.

Now convinced that he would be able to help, Dotty felt a spring in her step for the first time since this whole horrid business had started. She resisted the urge to break into a gallop until the temptation proved too much when she rounded the corner to face the long, straight corridor that led to her great-uncle's study. She took a bit of a run at it, and then jumped lightly onto the back of the trolley for a ride. The trolley popped a wheelie, slopping syrup across the tray and overturning the stack of pancakes, albeit that none fell on the floor – thank goodness for that.

Reaching her great-uncle's room, she knocked at the door. It was closed, which was unusual as Great-Uncle Winchester was in the habit of leaving the door open when he was in his office. There was no question of him being there though as Dotty could hear his booming voice inside, obviously talking to somebody, although she couldn't make out whom. Not receiving an immediate response, Dotty knocked again.

"Just one minute," the familiar voice shouted; and after a bit of shuffling Dotty's great-uncle swung the door open wide, ushering her and the trolley inside. Expecting to see that he had a visitor, Dotty was surprised to find that he was alone, with the exception of Geoff, who slobbered expectantly, clearly after a slice of bacon. Perhaps her great-uncle had been having a conversation with the dog. Geoff drooled hungrily. He, too, was looking decidedly cleaner following his recent bath at the hands of the gardener, Kenny. There seemed to be a lot of it going around.

"My dear girl, what can I do for you?" Great-Uncle Winchester said, breaking her out of her reverie.

"It's Joe," Dotty replied, instantly focused. "I wondered if you could help find him."

"Ah, yes, little Joe I heard about the misfortune of his disappearance. A terrible business indeed." Dotty was surprised to see that her great-uncle looked a bit down in the dumps.

"Yes, it is. Is there nothing you can do to find him? I mean, after all, you know the goings on of the sweeps. And you have a connection with the Council, don't you?"

"I understand your frustration," her great-uncle began, "but these are delicate matters. The Council has other serious issues to consider, and at present there is no saying what part Joe plays in all of them, if indeed there is any."

Dotty's disappointment turned to anger. This was no time for adult caution - her friend's life was at stake. "But you must be able to do something," she begged. "Pip told me what happened with that boy: Skitter, wasn't it? Can't he be made to talk? Can't you at least ask him if they have Joe? Surely he can tell you that much."

"We need to tread carefully, my dear. The Council..."

"I don't care about the Council!" Dotty cried. "And I don't care about their disappearing chimneys! I care about Joe! He's my friend. He's in danger, and we need to find him Right now!"

Dotty's voice rose. Geoff gave a small whimper and went to seek refuge under his master's writing desk.

"What would you do if it was me who was lost?" Dotty asked defiantly. "I know you are connected to the sweeps, and to the Council— that *we* are connected. But you've never explained to me how. I've lost my parents, my best friend, my whole life back in Cardiff; and I've been sent here to you and to Pip and to all of this mess! I've been hounded and chased and threatened and up and down chimneys, and there's been no proper explanation of any of this, except for you to tell me that you'd explain when I was big enough. Well, I am big enough. My friend is missing and I have a right to know."

"Darling girl, I do understand, but there are greater forces than you or I at play here." Her great-uncle shushed Dotty with a gesture as she drew herself up, ready for another outburst. "As it happens, I do have an idea. Let me speak with the Council and see what I can do. But you must leave it to me."

"Okay, Great Uncle Winchester," Dotty agreed grudgingly. "But when will you speak to them? When will you know?"

"As soon as I've finished my pancakes. Now run along; the syrup is at risk of getting cold, and I'd hate to see it wasted." He ushered her towards the study door, closing it behind her. Dotty felt suspicious. She was sure he was trying to get rid of her. "And, my dear, it's Winnie, if you please."

"Okay, Winnie," Dotty replied, as the door closed at her heels. "And thank you," she faltered through the solid oak door that was now shut between them.

Stops and Starts

Chapter 9

Solutions

In which Great Uncle Winchester hatches a plan

"My, she's a spirited one," the old man said to Geoff as the dog ventured out from his hiding place under the desk. "Yes, definitely a Winchester, that one. She'll make a good Guardian. Just like her mother."

"Right then, back to business," He scratched a spot behind Geoff's ear.. "Pip, dear boy! The coast is clear now, you can come out."

A pair of blackened, dirty feet dangled in the chimney opening, and then set down lightly in front of the grate. "She won't give up, you know," warned Pip. "She's like a dog with a bone."

"I know, boy, I know. But young Dorothea is right. We need to take matters in hand. And I think I have an idea that might just move our errant sweep, Skitter, into a more helpful frame of mind." The old man paused. "Go and tell the Council that I wish to convene an emergency meeting in…" he paused, eyeing the stack of pancakes, "…let's say, half an hour. Now off you go and be quick about it. My breakfast is spoiling."

"Yes Sir. Right away, Sir," Pip replied. And in a moment he was gone.

With Pip on his way, Winchester settled down to his mountain of pancakes, feeding one to a grateful Geoff, whilst he poured himself a now rather stewed cup of tea. He ate swiftly, clearing his plate and then, mopping up some stray syrup that had strayed onto one enormous sideburn, he slowly bent down to exchange carpet slippers for a battered old pair of brogues.

Striding over to the bookshelf to the right hand side of the fireplace, he ran his fingers along the rows of books, battered old copies of first editions, ancient and worn, until they reached the spine of a small book, bound in blue cloth and gilded with the name 'Kingsley' on it. He pulled the book forwards and stepped back, allowing the secret door to open. Once revealed, he surveyed the long teardrop-shaped passageway, its end sloping downwards, reaching far into the distance, beyond the study and the House.

"Geoff, my faithful hound, keep watch," instructed the old man, and he set off down the passageway and out of sight.

After a brisk ten-minute walk that took him along the length of the subterranean passage, Bartholomew Winchester finally reached his destination. The old man heaved aside the door to the great chamber. The door scraped uneasily against the stone floor that preceded it, creating echoes in the cavernous chamber that lay beyond.

There were already a number of people milling in the room, the chamber continuing to fill as Winchester entered it. He proceeded in taking his seat in the room, the awkward groaning of the stone door announcing his arrival. As he settled himself on the chair a neat and officious-looking sweep approached him, hailing him in greeting.

"I see that you are here, Council Master," the sweep gave a low bow. "We are almost all gathered, sir. Just a few more minutes and the Council will have a quorum."

Winchester nodded and, adjusting himself in his seat a little further, he sat and waited for the assembly of sweeps to finish filling the room. Some came in through a set of double doors on the far side of the hall, but the majority came down the vast chimney that sat centrally to the room, halfway along one wall to the left of the Council Master's chair.

The heavy marble surround shuddered at the weight of traffic it bore, as sweep after sweep landed on the empty stone hearth with a scuffle and a thud. But there were no collisions. With barely a stumble or a cough sweeps of all ages, male and female alike, entered the chamber in this way, filling the hall one after the other until almost every seat in the assembly was taken. As the last couple of sweeps took their seats, the sweep official once more approached Winchester, bowing again in reverence to the old man.

"Council Master, the assembly is ready for you now." As he bowed, the deferential aide's nose almost grazed the floor. "Sir: your brush." The man held out the solid symbol of office of the Sweeps' Council for Winchester to take.

The old man accepted the broom graciously. "Thank you, Sweetings," he replied. Then rapping the broom on the floor three times, he called the room to order.

As the striking of the brush rang out against the marble floor, a hush came over the room, all eyes on Winchester, watching him in quiet anticipation. "Greetings, all; I appreciate you coming at short notice," he began. "Now, if we are all assembled, let us bring in the boy."

"Can he stop our chimneys disappearing?" someone called out from the assembly.

"Yes, Council Master. We're all losing our livelihoods here," another hollered.

"Something needs to be done." a third shouted.

"Order." cried the Council Master, rapping the brush on the floor. "I will have order in this House."

"The boy is nothing but a common thief. What can he do to help?" yet another sweep interjected.

The Council Master looked severe. "We need to coax this boy into talking to us, no matter what our view of him. If he can lead us to the person who is plotting against us and closing our chimneys, he is more use to us than anyone else, in this room or otherwise."

A hush fell over the room. After a brief interlude, Skitter was once again brought into the chamber, escorted by the same two guards that had attended him in his last visit to the ballroom under the lake.

The ripples in the water above spread a dappled green light across the room, lighting up the faces of the assembly as they waited for the Council Master to address the prisoner. Now in the plain light of day it was evident to the waiting audience that the boy's troubled mind had not been helped by his recent incarceration. Still pitifully thin, the boy twitched and fidgeted, like a skittish horse bothered by a fly. His eyes danced around the room, searching, desperate. Was he still looking for a means of escape? Or was he searching for something else now; or someone else? A few gasps and assorted mutters echoed in the room.

Finally, Winchester spoke. "Skitter, I trust the Council have been keeping you well?"

The boy did not meet the Council Master's stare, his eyes still flitting round the room, searching for something. Winchester continued. "The guards say that you have been calling out from your cell, saying a name: a girl's name, Sarah."

This time the old man's words achieved the desired result. The boy's eyes snapped into focus, his steely gaze meeting the Council Master's at the mention of the name.

"Sarah!" he cried. "I must get out! My sister needs me. She is alone! In danger! She needs Skitter. Please! Let me out. LET - ME - OUT!" The disgraced sweep screeched out in his mental turmoil, wild now, a caged animal clawing frantically at his bonds. The guards fought to restrain him. There was a single sharp intake of breath from the gathered assembly at the perceived threat of his escape. Only Winchester seemed calm.

"Boy, you know as well as the Council that there is little chance of your release. You are a thief, a known consort of the Vagabond King: a man who poses a real and present danger to the Council and, besides, you are clearly unwell."

Skitter screamed in rage and frustration at the Council Master's words. The crowd gasped, but Winchester continued.

"Skitter, calm yourself. There is nothing you can do now." The Council Master raised his voice above the troubled boy's shrieks of displeasure. "But I believe, if you will let us, that there is a way in which we can help each other."

Solutions

Chapter 10
Through the
Window

In which Pip takes Dotty into the world beyond the
Calendar House

Pip sat cross-legged on Dotty's fireside rug, picking at a frayed edge while Dotty paced the room. She was still pretty cross at Pip for confiding in Sylv before her, but his promptness in bringing her the latest news had served to placate her a little.

"So tell me again, Pip."

"The Council have spoken to Skitter."

"That's the boy who used to be an apprentisweep like you, but got banned by the Council for stealing. Right?" Dotty interrupted.

"Yes," Pip confirmed. "And he has told us that the leader of his gang of thieves, this Vagabond King, is keeping a boy captive."

"So that must be Joe!" Dotty balled her fists in delight.

"Well, we hope so, yes."

"But that's amazing! I mean, the Council: they've really found him?"

"Well, not exactly: not yet." Pip spoke quickly now. "They know the gang has a boy, but they don't yet know where he is."

Dotty felt ready to burst, but Pip held a hand up, holding her back. "The Council has made a deal with Skitter. If they can find his sister, Sarah and make her safe, he will in exchange tell the Council where the Vagabond King is keeping Joe."

"So now we have someone else to find? Unbelievable," Dotty exploded. "And anyway, how can we trust this Skitter? He's a thief isn't he? What's to say we don't find his sister for him and then he just disappears off and we never get to know where Joe is."

"Skitter will never be released now; not after what he has done. On the streets his sister will either die of starvation or be picked up by a sweep trader and forced into slavery. He knows that his only hope of saving her is by allowing her into the Council's care. With luck, she will be adopted by a sweep family and given a kind and loving home. It is more than Skitter could have hoped for, even if he himself had been able to continue to look after her."

"But why won't he be released?" questioned Dotty. "I know he's been caught travelling where he shouldn't, and that he has a history of stealing, but surely that in itself isn't enough to keep him locked up forever?" She stared at Pip, hands on hips. "Is there something you're not telling me?"

Pip didn't answer. Dotty shrugged, exasperated. "I don't know. You're all as bad as each other. I only ever get half the story."

Pip ignored her.

Dotty huffed. "Fine. It doesn't matter now. We'd better get going."

"Oh no. You're not coming," said Pip.

"I am, you just try and stop me. Anyway, you need me."

"What would we need you for?" Pip resisted. "Why can't you just let the sweeps do it?"

Dotty glared at him. "Because Sarah is a little girl living in the shadows: without her brother and very much alone. She is going to be scared, especially of an apprentisweep like you. Don't you think that Skitter will have taught her to fear you after what happened to him?"

Pip stared at Dotty, arms crossed.

"So if I come with you, I can help gain her confidence; talk to her. Persuade her to come with us to safety," she finished.

"I still don't see why we need you."

Dotty rolled her eyes. "I suppose you could just take Sylv instead. You seem to prefer her to me."

"You always have to push it, don't you?" retorted Pip. "Look, I explained: you was asleep when I heard the news from the Council; otherwise I would have told you first. And besides, it's up to Mr Winchester's whether you can go. Not me."

"Fine," pouted Dotty. "Let's go and ask him then."

"Whatever you say, Miss," sighed Pip. "Come on then, oh feisty one," he said, giving her a playful jab in the ribs. "There's no time to lose. Mr Winchester's waiting in his study."

"A-ha! My intrepid explorer!" Dotty was pleased to see Great-Uncle Winchester greeting Pip with renewed gusto as they knocked at the open study door. "And Dorothea's waving you off, I see." He ushered them into the room.

"No, I'm going with him." Dotty was quick to put her great uncle straight. "My darling girl, it's too dangerous."

"And I'm not as little as you think. And besides, you need me. Sarah isn't going to go with an apprentisweep. Her brother will have taught her to fear them. You have to let me go." Dotty was firm.

Great Uncle Winchester pondered a moment. "So you think you can find this girl, Sarah? It's a very important job, you understand. She's the key, dear girl. The key to everything: to finding your friend Joe and to bringing down this band of vagabonds and their false King."

"Yes, I do know, Winnie," Dotty replied seriously. "Don't worry. We'll find her."

"That's settled then." Dotty's great uncle patted her a little too hard on the back, practically bowling her over with his enthusiasm. "But I want you to take Geoff with you. It could be dangerous."

Pip winced. "Sir, I really don't think we need…"

"Let me be the judge of that, Master Pip," interrupted Great-Uncle Winchester. "You might know the streets, but Miss Dorothea does not. Geoff is a faithful guard dog, and if you run into trouble you can send him to me for aid. Now, go on, the pair of you." He didn't wait for further argument from Pip. "The sooner we bring an end to this messy business, the better."

He strode over to his study window, opening the blind to the street beyond, and opened the sash.

With an agile leap, Pip hopped straight through the window and, once his feet were firmly planted the other side, held a hand out to Dotty. "Are you ready?"

"As I'll ever be," she replied, and taking his hand, hoisted herself up over the sill.

"Don't forget Geoff!" Great-Uncle Winchester called after them, puffing and blowing as he strained to lift Geoff's dead weight through the open window, the dog panting and wagging his tail as he struggled to get through.

"Unbelievable," Pip muttered under his breath.

With one last shove, Geoff fell through the window and at last was with them on the busy street beyond. Pip and Dotty waved a brief goodbye as Great Uncle Winchester closed the sash behind them and then turned as Dotty and her companions quickly disappeared into the crowd.

"Right." Pip was straight down to business. "The girl we are looking for is around six years old, but she will be small for her age, and thin. Dark hair, blue eyes – that's about the only information we have."

"Not much to go on, is it?" said Dotty.

"No, but I have a good idea of where to start looking, and there are a couple of people I can ask." Pip held Dotty's arm for a moment. "You okay?"

"Yes, I'm fine."

"Okay then, let's go."

Dotty followed Pip as he strode purposefully through the crowded market place, picking his way between stands and stalls, street performers and musicians, food sellers, pedlars and sweeps of all shapes and sizes going about their daily business. The whole place was teeming with life, and all around her Dotty could smell the scent of toil and sweat and horse manure and sweet rotting hay—along with the more inviting aroma of the many charcoal ovens dotted around the square. Street sellers called out to her as she passed their stalls, offering their wares in their own distinctive styles.

"Broom for your hearth, miss?"

"Roast chestnuts."

"Ribbons and lace."

"Hot potato, miss? Straight from the oven and hot buttered..."

Between the sights and the sounds, and the throng of busy people filling the walkways, Dotty had soon fallen behind the purposeful sweep and was at risk of losing him altogether. Geoff was still by her side, slowed down by the abundance of food opportunities that surrounded him, but Pip had gone on ahead and was almost out of sight. For a moment she lost him, but then saw his blond head bobbing in amongst the crowd. She called out after him "Pip! Hold on. Wait up."

Pip stopped and waited whilst Dotty picked her way through the crowd.

"Are you all right?" he asked her.

"Yes, fine," Dotty answered. "It's just that I don't know the town like you do and it's really crowded and, well, I don't know where we're going."

"We're going to the Tanneries," replied Pip in hushed tones. "It's the poorest part of the town - teeming with the homeless and the poor. If she's anywhere, she'll likely be there. You ready?"

"Yes," said Dotty.

"Good," he replied, "'cause I'm supposed to be finding a girl: not losing one. Mr Winchester would never forgive me."

"Hang on a minute," exclaimed Dotty. "Where's Geoff?"

It didn't take long to find the greedy spaniel. He had somehow managed to get hold of a sausage ring from one of the street stalls and was now trying to eat it. But the steaming sausage was too hot, so he kept on dropping it on the ground and then picking it up again, each time a little muddier and more grit-covered than it had been before.

"Pitiful," said Pip. "Why Mr Winchester puts so much store by that sorry state of a dog, I'll never know."

They both looked on, Dotty laughing, as Geoff choked down the last of the now extremely unappetising-looking sausage.

"Now, if you're both ready, can we please get going?" complained Pip. I want to get there before it gets dark and there's a fair bit of ground to cover. Dotty, stay close," he ordered. "I don't want you getting lost again."

"Yes, Sir," replied Dotty mockingly. But she picked up her pace, nonetheless.

As Dotty and a now very full Geoff followed Pip's brisk pace through the town, she soon became aware that they were no longer in the market square that filled the Calendar House courtyard, but had somehow moved beyond it. Rows of brightly-coloured canvas stalls had given way to streets and alleyways, lined on either side by buildings of brick and stone, and the cobbled courtyard was replaced by dirt roads, strewn with straw. Dotty was startled by the rumbling of wheels behind her and turned to see a covered cart bearing down on her, the single horse that pulled it blinkered and seemingly unaware of her presence.

Pip yanked her out of its path just in time. "Watch where you're going!" he scolded.

Shaken, but with no time to make a fuss, Dotty pressed onwards with Pip, now feeling a little less confident in her strange surroundings. They seemed to have been travelling for an awfully long time. They had reached a more gloomy area of the town.

As they walked, Dotty was aware of the alleyways becoming darker and narrower, the walkways more dirty and unkempt. Tattered awnings jutted out from faded shop fronts and children huddled in doorways, begging; sleeping, or just sitting. But there were no little girls of Sarah's description. Every so often, Pip and Dotty would stop, each asking any sympathetic face they could find for a clue as to Sarah's whereabouts.

"Have you seen a girl?"

"About so high."

"Dark hair, blue eyes."

"Her name is Sarah."

But to no avail. It was beginning to get dark. The shadows lengthened as they fought through the lines of washing that crisscrossed the streets; and Dotty could see that they were now entering the poorest part of the district. Geoff had moved closer to Dotty now. His soft coat brushed her leg as he padded along beside her. Dotty felt reassured by his presence.

Pip halted again, bidding Dotty wait as he went into a dimly-lit tavern to continue his enquiries. Dotty made to argue but Pip stopped her. "Not this one. It's too dangerous."

Dotty waited impatiently in the litter-filled alley. Geoff stood by her side, sniffing the air. For once he was bristling and alert, but that was far from a comfort for Dotty. She noticed a ragged curtain twitching behind cracked and dirt-ingrained glass. They were being watched. Dotty began to feel distinctly uneasy. Pip re-emerged from the dingy tavern, his expression signalling another failure. "Come on," he muttered. And so they trudged on.

As darkness fell, fires were lit in braziers in gaps between houses and in doorways and alleyways, producing flickering patches of light that threw shadows across their path as they walked. Dotty was getting hungry. They seemed to have been walking for miles. She wished she'd taken up one of the street sellers on their offer of food earlier in the day. Her stomach rumbled. Geoff whined in sympathy. "All right, boy," she patted his head reassuringly. "It won't be long now."

But Pip did not acknowledge their heavy hint for food, neither turning around nor breaking his pace.

Dotty halted. "Pip, Stop!"

He turned and his expression gave Dotty her answer without her needing to ask the question. The search was not looking good.

"So what now?" she asked him. "Most people won't even talk to me, let alone tell anything else."

"Mrs Scritch," replied Pip, looking grave. "It's the only option we have left."

Pip's expression left Dotty feeling alarmed. She didn't like the sound of this person at all, whoever she was. And it was patently clear that Pip wasn't the woman's greatest fan, either.

"So who's Mrs Scritch?"

"She's the proprietor of the Tanneries Orphanage."

"Do you think Sarah might have been taken in, then? But that's a good thing, isn't it?"

"Not the way Mrs Scritch runs things, no," replied Pip sourly. "Come on, it's not much further." He beckoned her to follow.

They walked for several more minutes, all the while Dotty turning over in her mind Pip's comment about Mrs Scritch and her orphanage. She didn't know what he could mean, but she was sure of one thing: if Pip didn't like the woman, Dotty was sure that she would like her even less.

At last they reached the darkened side street that was their destination, lit only by a single lamp that hung from a bracket on the street corner. The light reached its yellow fingers into the alley a short way, but the passage end was obscured by shadow.

"Down here." Pip ushered her in.

The crumbling building that he led her to was in a sorry state. There had once been a lantern over the doorway but it had long since broken, its glass smashed and ragged in its rusty frame. The steps up off the street were uneven and cracked, the iron handrail rotted and broken. To the right of the unlit doorway Dotty could just make out the letters of a peeling sign, old and faded, the corner ripped and missing. It said: *The Tanneries Orphanage: home for waifs and strays.* The whole place looked hopelessly uncared for.

"I hope they look after their children better than they do their building," Dotty remarked.

She mounted the steps and gave a firm rap at the door. The wood sounded hollow and rotten to Dotty, as if too much knocking might break it. At first there was no answer but then, after a few minutes of persistent hammering, the door creaked open an inch, leaving just enough room for a small eye to survey the party that stood on the doorstep.

"Good evening," Dotty spoke gently to the child. "Mrs Scritch, if you please."

The child did not speak but scampered back off into the house, presumably to fetch his mistress. They waited. After a few minutes and some muffled shouting, Dotty heard footsteps approaching the door. Presently, the door opened a crack further to reveal a scrawny-looking woman standing in the doorway.

"Mrs Scritch, I see that you are home," greeted Pip.

"Where else am I going to be?" the woman snapped, showing a mouthful of rotten teeth. "What do you want? Did the Council send you?" she continued, her tone less than friendly.

"We are looking for a girl," continued Pip, undeterred.

"Around six years of age," Dotty chimed in. "Small, dark, goes by the name Sarah. We wondered if you might know where she is."

"There's no Sarah here," replied Mrs Scritch tartly, moving to shut the door.

Pip took a step forward, blocking the entranceway and preventing her from doing so. Mrs Scritch clasped the door edge with bony fingers, trying to somehow slam it shut. "And besides," she said to Pip, "isn't one girl enough for you?" The objectionable woman pointed a broken nail at Dotty.

"The Council pays you well, Mrs Scritch," Pip stated baldly. "You get a fine price for the children you take in off the streets. It is only unfortunate that you seem to 'lose' so many of them."

"You know full well they run away," retorted the woman. "They are street urchins and beggars, most of them, and they crave a life on the streets with the rats and the dirt and all that they are used to. No amount of wholesome food and warm hearth can persuade them to stay here."

"To the contrary, Mrs Scritch, I know full well that they do not run away, although given your pitiful treatment of them who would blame them if they did." Pip challenged.

"I wonder what the Council would have to say if they had word that you are doing a nice little trade in children on the side; lining your pockets with the ill-gotten monies of the sweep traders?" joined in Dotty.

Pip glanced sideways at Dotty, looking impressed. Dotty gave a small smile back. The moment quickly passed as Pip had to fight with Mrs Scritch to keep the door ajar.

"Oh yes, Mrs Scritch," he smirked at her. "I daresay they might have something to say about that."

"You wouldn't dare!" shrieked Mrs Scritch. "Just try it. And see what will happen to you, *Apprentisweep*. Be gone with you. You and your little *friend*."

Geoff made a move away from Dotty now. With his front paws on the top step, he emitted a low growl of warning, daring Mrs Scritch to lay a hand on her.

Dotty could see that for all her talk the woman was scared of the Council and she was sure Mrs Scritch had some information on Sarah. She decided to try her luck. "I could be wrong of course, but I'll wager you have more to lose than me, Mrs. So why don't you just tell us what we need to know," she demanded. Dotty crossed her fingers behind her back and waited while the woman considered her options.

After a short internal wrestle the woman spoke again. "I don't know of no Sarah," she answered sulkily. "But there is a girl meets your description down Squabblers Yard. You could try there. We invited her into the warmth and comfort of our home, of course, but she couldn't be persuaded."

"Can't think why not," muttered Dotty.

"Thank you, Mrs Scritch," said Pip, taking Dotty by the elbow and steering her away from the doorstep and down the alley, heading for the darkness, rather than back out into the dimly-lit street beyond.

As they went on their way, Mrs Scritch continued to shout after them, "Don't think you've heard the end of this, Sweep! That's the last favour you ask of me. Mark my words..."

Smiling silently at each other, Dotty and Pip left her screaming her fury into the night and hurried off together into the dark.

When she had first saw it Dotty had assumed that the alley was a dead end and so she was surprised that Pip had led them that way, and even more so to find that it led into quite a wide open space between the overcrowded tenements.

"What is this place?" she asked Pip, her voice hushed. "It gives me the creeps."

"This is Squabblers Yard," he replied. "It's where we're going to find Sarah."

Dotty could see now that the break in the buildings was the result of the collapse of some larger building or block of buildings. The clearing was filled with rubble in between which were makeshift dwellings where the poorest of the poor had made their homes. An open sewer ran down the middle of the street and Dotty and Pip had to watch their step for fear of finding themselves ankle deep in filth.

Dotty looked on in despair. "How are we going to find her?" she asked.

"We'll find her," replied Pip resolutely.

They started to pick through the jumble of makeshift huts and crudely-made shanty dwellings, searching for Skitter's unfortunate sister. To be faced with such utter poverty and hopelessness was almost more than Dotty could bear. Her lip trembled and she had to stop herself from crying at the sight of the poor folk that lived in this strange town that somehow existed within the walls of the Calendar House. How could her great uncle have let this happen? Was there nothing he could do? Did he even care? And they still couldn't find Sarah.

But just as they were about to give up their search, Dotty noticed Geoff pawing at something in a dark corner. The spaniel was eagerly sniffing at an old bundle of rags wedged in between two boxes and an overflowing bin, the bin spewing its rotted remains out on to the mud.

"Come away, Geoff," Dotty scolded. "It's just a pile of dirty rags. There's nothing in there for you."

But Geoff was persistent. He started whining, making Dotty suspicious. "Pip," she called. "I think Geoff might have found something."

Pip was quickly at the scene. "It's nothing. The old dog probably just smelled a rat."

Whatever it was, Geoff wasn't going to leave it alone. He pawed and whined at the bundle, his tail wagging at his discovery. Dotty squinted more closely. And then in the fading light she saw it: in amongst the threadbare rags there was a face. It was a small girl, with dark hair and dark eyes, and skin as pale as porcelain that shone in the moonlight, giving away her hiding place in amongst the trash.

Dotty spoke as soothingly as she could muster, although she felt far from calm. "Hi, there," she said. "I'm Dotty. And you must be Sarah."

The little girl recoiled at the mention of her name, fearful of being discovered.

"Don't worry," Dotty soothed. "We're here to help. We know your brother, Skitter."

"Skitter?" The girl gave a faint smile, but then she seemed to lose consciousness.

"Quickly," said Dotty. "Pip, help me. I think she's ill."

Together the two unwrapped from around her the stinking rags that hid the girl's delicate frame. Even as they unravelled the cloth Dotty could see that she was shaking like a leaf, her eyes flickering as her surroundings faded in and out of vision.

"She has a fever," said Pip. "We need to get her to the Council straight away."

As they pulled the last of the rags from her body, Dotty was surprised to see that her tiny legs were encased in metal calipers. The girl was obviously a cripple. Pip lifted her into his arms with ease. She was too insensible to protest and, even if she had been coherent, she was too weak to struggle. In that instant, Dotty was reminded of a starling chick that she had once rescued after it had fallen out of its nest onto the path in her small back garden at her old home on Wyvern Road.

"She wouldn't have lasted another night here," Pip said solemnly. "It's lucky we found her."

Dotty nodded, a bit lost for words.

"Right, quick sharpish, we'd better get her back to Mr Winchester before it's too late."

"But I thought you needed to get her to the Council?" Dotty said.

"Yes, we do. But, for now, the Calendar House is the best place for her," replied Pip. "She'll be safest there."

Dotty was confused by Pip's explanation, but the matter was clearly too urgent to stand about arguing so she kept her questions for later. Quickly the pair retraced their steps through the Tanneries. With Geoff beside them and their precious cargo in Pip's arms, they raced through the night back to the safety of more brightly-lit streets and to the warmth and comfort of the Calendar House.

Through the Window

Chapter 11

Captives

In which Joe meets his captor and discovers that he is not the only captive in a cage.

Joe was awakened by a noise coming from the chimney. By now he was used to the chimney bearing unwelcome visitors, or one at least: his gaoler the magpie. But this noise was different. It was bigger and somehow more threatening.

The noise increased and the chimney breast began to shudder, red dust shaking out from the brickwork, the mortar cracking and splintering. Joe had a sense that the chimney was struggling to contain, not just something of great size, but something of great power as it descended. Instinctively he backed into the corner of his cage farthest from the fireplace, knees hugged tightly to his chest, his breathing shallow and quick. There was a rumble growing in the chimney like the echo of a thunderstorm approaching at full speed. Joe held his breath in fear of what was to come.

With one final shudder the chimney spat out its cargo. It was a man: tall and powerfully built, but light on his feet, evident from the way he landed almost cat-like in the open grate. The magpie followed quickly behind, coughing and spluttering and shedding its untidy feathers as the man drew himself up to his full height, adjusting his great coat and brushing soot from his cuff.

From the corner of his cage, Joe watched the man, terrified, surveying the man's long black hair and dark complexion, his eyes like deep pits leading to his black heart, or who knew where else. Could this be the King of whom the bird had spoken? Surely not. He wore no crown or royal robes. To the contrary, his beaten and dirty top hat and threadbare clothes gave away no sign of nobility or riches. His thick black boots were well-worn and his neckerchief was torn; and the heavy woollen coat that sat across his broad shoulders had been patched so many times that it looked like a homespun quilt. But he exuded from his being such force and strength that Joe could not mistake this for anything but a man with huge power: an ancient power, borne not of kingly kindness or mercy or grace, but of steel and grit and determination.

The man carried something in his hand. At first Joe thought from its size and shape that it must be a lantern. But there was no light coming from its centre, and a dirty brown rag covered it. The cloth reminded Joe of the cover his mother put over Eric the budgerigar's cage at night. It could be a bird house, Joe supposed. But he could not hear a noise from inside, unless of course it was empty. Joe wondered for a moment if it might belong to the magpie. But no - it was certainly far too small for that.

The man sat down heavily at the table, placing the cage on top of it. "Mordecai, my wine," he barked an order at the bird, who got straight to work, taking the metal flagon from the table and hopping over to a dusty barrel that sat in the corner of the room to fill it with dark red liquid.

It was the first time Joe had heard the bird's name: Mordecai. It seemed strange to him that he had been in the magpie's company all this time and yet he hadn't known this simple fact about it. He wasn't sure that the bird knew Joe's name either, for that matter.

The man took a long slow draught of his wine and then, wiping spilt liquid from his chin with the back of his hand he turned, his attention focusing on the boy.

"Now you're a pretty little problem, aren't you my lad?"

"Let me out," Joe cried. "You big bully!"

"And you're a feisty little problem too, I see," laughed the man, although there was no humour in his voice.

Mordecai sprang suddenly into action, falling over his clawed feet to get to Joe's cage, his mechanical eye staring at Joe, whizzing and clicking. "Respect the King, bow to the King. Fear the King!" he shrieked through the bars, his sharp beak snapping at Joe as it spoke. Joe recoiled. He had never seen the magpie that worked up before. He wasn't sure whether he was more scared of him or the strange man who sat at the table.

"Calm yourself, Mordecai," the man spoke again "The boy will learn to fear me soon enough, if he doesn't already." He turned to Joe, his steely gaze reached into the cage, drawing Joe towards his bottomless pits of eyes with some unknown force or magnetism. "It seems I have forgotten my manners," he said. "You have given me your name, Joe. It is only fitting that I should give you mine." His lips smiled a cold smile that failed to reach his eyes. "They call me the Vagabond King," he said, putting one hand across his chest, his head nodding in a feigned show of deference.

Joe shivered, but his attentions were distracted by a sudden movement from the cage that sat on the table top. It shook slightly, and then rocked from side to side as if its inhabitant was trying to topple it.

"Quiet," the man growled, his hand slamming down on the top of the cage, bidding it to be still. There was a small high-pitched scream of displeasure from within: definitely not a bird. Whatever could it be?

"This one's feisty too, although not as pretty as you are," the man addressed Joe, patting the top of the cage none too gently with a huge powerful hand. More high-pitched chattering emitted from underneath the brown cloth, the cage's occupant clearly was not pleased. The cloth billowed out at one side for a moment, as whatever lay underneath it gave it a kick through the bars.

Joe stared at the dirty rag.

"Want to know what it is, do you?" he leered at Joe, leaning towards him. "Want to find out what I've got tucked away under this cloth?"

Joe stared, his fear paralysing him. He managed a shadow of a nod.

"No, Master!" shrieked Mordecai. "Don't show the boy. It's dangerous."

The bird tried to put himself between his master and the cage, but the King simply knocked him aside. "Out of my way, impudent bird!" he bawled, throwing the cover off the cage.

Joe stared at its contents. He rubbed his eyes in disbelief. It was a tiny person. Well, sort of. It was person-like, in that it had arms and legs and a body and a head. But it was small and dark and leathery and wizened, as if it had been dunked in muddy water for too long and then shrivelled like a dirty brown prune. The King had been right about that at least – the occupant of the cage definitely wasn't pretty. Ugly as it was, though, the creature was no less fascinating. Joe realised now that the muffled squeaks he'd heard had been the creature speaking, although not in any language Joe understood.

He edged forwards to the front of his own cage, trying to get a better look. Mordecai flapped about squawking his distress, but both man and boy ignored him.

"Say what that is, can you, boy?" the man asked, smirking at Joe. "Well?" he snapped, not giving Joe a chance to answer. "Can you, eh?"

Joe stared. He could only think that it had to be some sort of spirit, some mystical being that the King had trapped. He wracked his brains. He had heard his grandmother talk of jinns, but he had imagined them to be quite different than this. Could this be one of the mischievous spirits of which she spoke? Feeling less than sure, he offered the only answer he had at that moment, which was "N...n...no, sir, I can't."

"Ha! I knew it!" exclaimed the King, seemingly pleased at Joe's ignorance. "This, my lad, is a hob: the most ancient and powerful of faerie folk. Taken by my very own hand from the hearth it inhabited. And very useful it has proved, too."

He chuckled to himself, but Joe didn't see the joke.

"Ah, yes, it has served me well. And you will do well for me too, Joe. By the time I've finished with you, you'll be worth a thousand treacherous hobs if I'm not much mistaken." The man took another draught of his wine. "And do you know why, young Joe? Because whilst my little captive, the hob here, gives me the magick to close the chimneys of you ordinary folk one by one, you, boy, hold the key to something much more valuable."

Joe did not understand.

The man went on. "I have to admit to being angry with Skitter when he brought you to me. Foolish child; driven by panic to kidnap you after you made all that commotion when he came down your chimney. Making a right racket he said you was, threatening to call the police and all sorts. Almost woke the girl sleeping in the next room. Your sister, was it? Hmph." The man paused, eyeing Joe carefully.

Joe cried out as a sudden pain seared through his head, the full memory of his kidnapping rushing back to him. The fragments of memory that had haunted him since the night of his capture now flooded into his brain, all at once, showing him for the first time the full story of his abduction.

He remembered being woken by a noise coming from the chimney in his bedroom at home in Wyvern Road. He looked across to see if his sister Jazz was awake, but she was sleeping. All of a sudden there was a boy in the room, searching for something amongst Joe's things. He got out of bed, wanting to scream, to call for his parents, for the police. But the boy attacked him, grabbing him, bidding him to be quiet.

The boy was bigger than Joe, and older, and Joe was no match for him, roused from sleep as he was, and in the pyjamas that he still wore now. He struck out wildly, grabbing for anything he might use as a weapon, but the only thing on his bedside table was a small wind-up alarm clock and the paperback he was reading. He grabbed the clock and hit the boy in the temple with it as hard as he could, making the boy's head bleed. But the boy seemed not to notice and, wiping a trickle of blood from his eye as if it was nothing, he grabbed Joe in a steely grip and dragged him towards the chimney.

"Yes, at first it is true that I was at a loss what to do with you," the man went on, ending Joe's rêverie.

"You could have let me go," Joe retorted angrily.

"Ha! Yes, that would have been a fine thing, now wouldn't it? A fitting example for a king to set his people. To the contrary, I had in mind to make an example of you. A warning to those who would try to stall the attempts of the Vagabond King to restore order to the realms of magick folk and shut out the petty meddlers in your ordinary world that would trifle with us and our magicks. But as it turns out you were quite the lucky find, weren't you?" the King continued. "It seems Skitter was under the influence of a dose of his own sweep's luck that day. Or maybe that luck was yours, eh?"

The man laughed a sinister laugh that chilled Joe to the bone. He hesitated, frightened to speak with the man. "But I am not lucky," he faltered. "I am just a boy."

The Vagabond King laughed more heartily, slapping his thigh. "Just a boy indeed, young Joe: but a boy with influence, as it turns out."

"I.. I'm afraid I don't understand."

"Miss Parsons. Dorothea. Heir to the Winchester fortune. She is your friend, is she not?" the King huffed impatiently.

"Dotty?" the boy asked, surprised. "But what does she have to do with...?"

"Ha! You know nothing, do you, boy." The man settled back in his chair. "Your friend, 'Dotty', as you call her, as it happens is someone with whom I am most keen to become acquainted."

"But why?"

"Quiet, boy!" barked the man, "and I will tell you." Suddenly his hand shot out from under his greatcoat, reaching through the bars and grabbing Joe by his nightshirt front. He pulled him up to the bars, his jaw forced painfully against the cold metal, their faces almost touching. Joe felt the man's breath on his cheek and saw his black teeth, too close for comfort. He tried to pull back, but the man held him fast.

"Joe, you are a pawn, a chip, a prize to be bargained with," he snarled. "You see my boy, Skitter, came across an interesting piece of information recently, given to him by a man named Poachling with whom he has the fortune to share his current place of, er, residence. It seems your friend Dotty has something I want: a key of sorts. And I'll wager she'd hand it over in a flash, for the promise of your safe return."

He laughed heartily now, releasing Joe, letting him fall hard back onto the cold earth floor beneath him. "If only I'd known that little jewel of information earlier, I would have been saved a whole world of trouble! Aye," he chuckled, "if I'd known that, I would have stopped my searching and engineered Skitter's capture a long time ago."

"So, you see, lad, now I have two captives in a cage." boasted the man. "And together you will both bring me what I need to finish my plan."

The hob cursed and spat at his captor, fighting against the bars and shrieking its disdain as loudly as its tiny lungs would allow.

"Quiet, now," the King ordered the screaming faerie, pulling the dirty rag back over the cage to muffle the noise. But the creature continued to shriek at the top of its lungs.

Recovering himself, Joe flung himself back at the bars in despair. "Leave Dotty alone! I don't know anything about any keys, but she'll never agree to your demands. She'd leave me here to rot before she'd fall in with the likes of you!"

"Fine words, my boy," laughed the man. "You know, I like you, Joe. You're strong for one so small, and spirited. Perhaps, if you're right, I can make use of you in our band of thieves once this is all over. What say you to a life with me and my merry band?"

"I'd rather die, sir, than spend a single night in your company of vagabonds," Joe countered bravely.

"Very well, then. I see you are not to be dissuaded – for now. In that case you had better hope your Dotty is a better friend to you than you think." The man was serious now. "But there is time enough for such things. For now I have more urgent matters to attend to. There is the matter of some chimneys to close."

For some reason, this last comment gave rise to yet more angry shrieks from the direction of the covered cage that still sat on the table where the man had left it. But the King continued to ignore it.

"Come, Mordecai. We must away." The man got up from his chair, draining the last of his wine from the flagon and slamming it down on the table top. "It seems we have a bargain to strike."

The bird came to attention, fussing and scraping as its master strode towards the chimney breast. "Yes, Master. Of course, Master. But what about the creature?" It pointed a grimy wing towards the table.

"We have no need of it for the present task, Mordecai," replied the man. "I am minded to leave it here. I grow tired of its constant chattering. And it strikes me that my two captives may provide some company for each other in my absence."

"But Master, are you sure it be wise to leave it alone with the boy, sir? Hobs be dangerous, sir." The bird simpered, clearly nervous of its master.

"Would you question me, bird?" the King thundered. "Of course it is wise. I have the hob's name. There is no magick it can do in my absence that can harm me."

"But, Master..."

"Be done with your questions, Mordecai. That is enough." He silenced the bird with a hand. " Boy, I bid you farewell."

"But until when will you be gone?" Joe asked. "How long must I stay here?"

"I will be gone until I have need of you again," was the man's reply.

"Please don't go!" Joe pleaded. "I am frightened to be left here alone with the creature. And I have questions."

"Questions. Ha! You too presume to question me, do you?" The king cast a threatening glance at the magpie, who shuffled awkwardly from foot to foot, his head bowed low. "Don't worry, boy. You will understand in the fullness of time. Mark my words: you will. And besides, I leave you a little friend to play with. See?" He smiled grimly, roughly pulling the cover off the hob's cage.

"But..." Joe trailed off, because as he spoke the Vagabond King turned on his heel and, with a swish of his greatcoat, promptly left the building; leaving Joe and the hob alone.

Captives

Chapter 12

The Hob's

Secret

In which Joe and the faerie become acquainted and Joe is given an unexpected taste of home

Soon after the Vagabond King had gone, the hob fell silent, turning its back on Joe and seating itself on the floor of its cage. Joe watched at first with interest. But the creature remained still. And so, after some time had passed, weary of staring at the lifeless exhibit on the table, he drifted off into a fitful sleep. He didn't know how much later it was when he awakened but, as was often the case these days, it was a noise that roused him, though the source of the sound was not the chimney this time: it was the hob.

"*Psst!*" it whispered through the bars. "*Pssst!*"

"Hello?" replied Joe, hesitantly.

To his surprise, the hob answered in English. "Jo-oe," it called in a little singsong voice. "Oh Jo-ey. What a pretty name," it teased, turning around to face him, and allow its long brown nose to poke out through the bars.

Joe thought it strange to hear the hob speaking in English, but he welcomed the conversation from someone other than Mordecai, even if the hob was teasing him.

"It's short for Johd. It's Arabic," he explained, "but everyone just calls me Joe." There was something in the faerie's voice that made Joe suspicious, guarded. It sounded, well, somehow unkind. But for now he continued politely. "And what should I call you?"

There was a furious shriek from the hob's cage, followed by much hissing and spitting.

"Er, sorry; did I say something wrong?" Joe was keen to avoid another scene from the little creature like the ones he had witnessed earlier.

"A faerie's name is secret! You should never ask it," the creature scolded him.

"Oh," replied Joe. "I'm sorry – I didn't know that."

"There is great power in a name," it hissed. "You should not give yours away so lightly to strangers. After all, look at me," it demanded indignantly.

"Did you give the Vagabond King your name, then?" Joe asked.

"Give? Pah! No. More like someone gave it to him," the faerie said. "And whoever it was, they had better wish that I never find out *their* name, that's for sure."

And in that moment Joe fervently believed the creature, and wished with all his heart that he never had the misfortune to discover it.

"So what is it that he made you do?" Joe asked. "The King said you had been of use to him in closing chimneys. Why would he want to do that?"

"Tee, hee, hee!" the faerie chuckled with a sudden wicked glee that surprised Joe. "That fool, who calls himself King. He presumes to take magic from faerie; an ancient hob. He is vain indeed to think that he can outsmart me."

"Why?" asked Joe, feeling alarmed. "What have you done?"

The hob chuckled gleefully again. "Why, I have given him exactly what he wanted. He wants people's chimneys to disappear, and I have given him the magick to make that happen...just not in the way that he thinks!" It tittered appreciatively at its own private joke.

Joe's head reeled: faeries, magick, disappearing chimneys and now this. "I'm afraid I still don't understand," he told the Hob. "Why ever would he want to remove peoples' chimneys?"

"Remove! Ha!" the hob chuckled. "I see you make the same mistake as he! The King of the

Vagabonds wishes to close all the portals between this world and the world of the sweeps. And so he demands my magick to make the hearths disappear. Disappear they will, to the eyes of fools and sweeps. But what I have given him is nothing more than a simple glamour: the chimneys themselves remain!"

"A glamour?" asked Joe. "So it's just a trick? The chimneys appear sealed, but are still remaining?"

"You are sharp-witted for one so young. Yes, it is the very same glamour that makes faeries appear to children like pretty winged fireflies on a summer's eve. You humans are so woefully dependent on your eyes that you ignore your other senses."

Joe sat on his haunches, taking it all in. He looked at the hob, all brown and wrinkled. It was right – it was neither winged nor delicate, as the fairies of his pictures books showed.

"So fairies don't really look like that then?" he asked.

"Of course not!" scolded the hob. "They look as I do. The glamour simply makes us more pleasing to your human senses – so greedy for all that is beautiful you cannot see within. And that is exactly why nobody will see past the glamour that is being put upon the chimneys, even when it is there in front of them! The poor, dim-witted fools will not think to explore their lost chimneys; they will simply believe what their dull eyes tell them is the truth, and look no further. Until the spell wears off, of course. They deserve everything they get, really," it finished smugly.

Joe was horrified. "But what will happen when he finds out that you've tricked him? When the spell wears off, won't you be in real danger?"

"Oh he will find out before that," the hob grinned, "for I intend to tell him. And then I will make a bargain for the return of my name in exchange for the magick he truly desires."

Whilst the hob chuckled darkly to itself there came a familiar rustle in the chimney that Joe had come to recognise as the approach of his gaoler, Mordecai, bringing the morning rations. At once the hob fell silent, turning its back on Joe once again.

But the magpie's mechanical eye was apparently quick to see the movement on the table and it turned to Joe, clicking and whirring and flapping and fluttering in alarm. "Has the hob spoken to ye?" the bird asked, peering through the bars to Joe's cage.

"Y...yes," said Joe.

"What did it say?" quizzed his gaoler, leaning further into Joe's cage, his beak poking through the bars.

"It was me that spoke to him. I, er, asked it its name."

The bird squawked with fright, feathers shedding all over the floor. "Its name? It be surprising you is still here then, boy!"

"It wasn't pleased," Joe agreed.

Mordecai seemed placated, settling its untidy feathers a little. "So you spoke not further, then?" he asked.

"No. Well, yes: we chatted a little," admitted Joe.

"A very useful little chat," chimed in the mischievous hob.

"What?" Suddenly the bird was all alarm again, pacing about the room in a dither. "I told the Master. I warned him," the bird muttered to himself. "Foolish. Foolish! A hob would not bother with such a lowly creature as ye, unless it saw use in ye."

The hob hissed angrily at the bird. Mordecai snapped his sharp beak towards it, making the hob squeal with rage. With one swoop of his powerful beak the bird pushed the cage to the far corner of the table on which it sat.

Turning to Joe, Mordecai now spoke with urgency. "Tell me this boy: of what did ye speak? Did it ask anything of ye?"

"No," replied Joe, quite unnerved by the bird's obvious concern. "It didn't ask me anything. Honestly."

Joe's answer seemed to satisfy his gaoler for now. "Ye've been lucky, is all I have to say. Hobs are a race of power and one 'at can't be trusted. You'll leave well alone if you know what's good for ye, boy. Do not speak to it again lest you be tricked into a bargain with it!"

"No, sir, I won't."

"And so I bid ye farewell," said Mordecai. "I have an errand to run for the King. Be wary," he gave Joe his final warning and stalked back to the chimney.

With Mordecai gone, Joe looked at the unappetising crust of bread and stale, hard cheese that was his morning's ration. He thought it only polite to share it with the hob, which was now busy talking to itself in its own peculiar tongue, but it refused his portion of the food, blowing a raspberry at Joe when he offered.

"There's no need to be rude, you know," Joe snapped. Between Mordecai and the faerie he was getting pretty fed up with treading on eggshells for one morning. "It wasn't me that said you were untrustworthy – it was the bird." Sullenly he bit into the wedge of bread, wishing with all his heart for a taste of his mother's home cooking.

The hob appeared to repent of his impolite behaviour as it lifted a corner of the cloth that covered it and eyed Joe seriously. "Perhaps you are undeserving of your treatment," it conceded. "Such hardship is difficult for one of such tender years. Tell me, young Joe, what you like to eat at home."

It didn't take Joe long to think of an answer as it was the very thing he had been thinking of. "*Noon'o panir'o moraba*," he muttered, almost to himself, thinking of his mother's flat breads fresh out of the oven, topped with lashings of feta cheese and home-made quince jam.

The hob nodded sagely and, doing something with its hands that Joe couldn't make out, it breathed across its palm and out into the room in the direction of Joe's cage, almost like it was blowing a kiss. For a small moment it smiled. "You're welcome," it said.

"For wha..." Joe was in the middle of asking, when he looked down at his hands and almost dropped his breakfast. For he was no longer holding the stale crust of bread and cheese that his gaoler had brought for him; rather he was holding a warm, fresh slice of lavash bread, dripping with crumbly cheese and topped with sweet, sticky quince. The smell was almost too much for Joe and he swooned visibly, barely finding the words to utter a 'thank you' to his benefactor. He went to take a bite of bread, but then stopped himself, suspicious. "You haven't really turned my food into – well, this, have you?"

"No," the hob said chuckling. "It is but a simple glamour: a trick for the senses. You are still eating the same stale food that was given to you by the bird, but I think you will find your taste buds sufficiently tricked not to know the difference."

Joe was amazed. It even smelled like the food his mother baked for his family. He felt a sudden pang of longing for his mum and dad.

Closing his eyes, he bit into the bewitched bread. The faerie was right. It tasted every bit as good as if it was real.

"So now, at least, you understand the effectiveness of a faerie's glamour," the hob said with an air of satisfaction. "Works on you humans every time."

When Joe had finished eating, licking every last remnant of the sticky quince jam from his fingertips, he wanted to ask the hob again about the magic it had performed. But the faerie was busy in its cage, rocking from side to side again, trying to gain enough momentum to shift the heavy iron frame. Now that Mordecai had shifted it to rest on the very edge of the table, this had become less of the fruitless task that it had been when the hob had first arrived.

Slowly, Joe watched as the cage began, first to move and then to rock and shift at the table's edge. As the faerie's frantic efforts gained strength, Joe realised that it meant to knock its prison off the table, and he shouted out in fright, for fear that the hob would hurt itself. "Take care!" he called, like a spectator in a dangerous sport. "Watch out! You will be injured!"

But the hob paid no notice of Joe's warnings. Clearly, it wanted to be free.

After what seemed like an age the cage finally toppled, dropping off the table and hitting the floor so hard that it bounced, rolling haphazardly across the room until it crashed into the wall in a far corner.

"Are you all right?" shouted Joe. He saw that the metal bars had twisted and that the door had sprung open and lay hanging off its hinges. "Hob?" Joe called in alarm.

"Never fear, I am safe," a voice came from above him.

Joe looked up. The hob was hovering above the bars of Joe's pen, smiling once more. He would have said the hob was flying, except that it didn't have any wings.

"Forgive me," it said. "I needed to stretch my, er, well you know what I mean." It smiled a crooked little smile. "But now I must be off."

"What?" Joe spluttered. "You are leaving me here alone?" A blind panic swept over him, the like he had not felt since he had first arrived in the dark cellar room. "Please, won't you free me too? Surely you can – with magick?"

"I'm afraid I cannot," the faerie replied. "As you have just witnessed, picking locks is not a speciality of my species. And besides, without my name my powers are diminished. It is why you see me as you do. There is only so much I can achieve without it."

"But...there must be something you can do?" protested Joe. "I beg you!"

"Even if there was, little Joe, what would be the point?" said the hob, almost taunting him. "There are no doors in this room. The chimney is the only exit. So unless you can fly, or possess chimney magick, you will have no way out."

The truth hit Joe hard. The hopelessness of his situation engulfing him, he sank to the floor.

"Farewell, Joe," said the Hob.

Joe watched it heading for the open chimney, his mind desperately scrabbling round for a solution. But then, just before the hob darted out of sight, Joe called it back, shouting "Wait. Stop. Please! I think there is a way you can help."

Chapter 13
The Delivery

In which an unusual package comes down Dotty's chimney

Mordecai left the dank cellar that had become home to Joe, flying up through the ancient stone chimney and out into the chill, wet air. It was a cold morning. The wind was up and the sky was filled with billows of slate grey cloud, threatening a storm.

As the bird flew it began to rain; at first a little but then in great sheets, driven sideways by the wind. He beat his great wings, rallying against the volleys of rain that buffeted him. But birds are far more at home in the sky than on the ground, and Mordecai easily navigated the weather. Besides, he had been given a job to do for the King and the needs of his master transcended any storm.

The huge bird flew high into the atmosphere, rising above the great nimbus clouds to avoid the worst of the squall. Up here his movement was more confident than on the ground. He was a force to be reckoned with, in every sense a king of his own kind. Through breaks in the cloud Mordecai navigated over hills and dales, through rocky outcrops and finally past train lines and cityscapes until he reached the bare open countryside again and the moorland beyond. His dull, white, sightless eye was untroubled by the turbulent skies, but the mechanical appendage that he wore strapped across his head like a giant clockwork eyepatch buzzed and whirred, the lens zooming in and out as it struggled against the rain to focus on the landscape below.

At last it saw what it was looking for: a vast sprawling house with a central courtyard, standing alone on the moor like a huge stone sentinel, or an elaborate stone cake fit for a mountain troll. Lightning streaked across the sky, illuminating the Calendar House in sharp white relief against the backdrop of the bleak Yorkshire landscape that surrounded it.

Mordecai gave a triumphant croak, descending rapidly through the breaking banks of cloud whilst, from his brass eye, a red light scanned the endless rooftops in search of a chimney. At last the bird spotted his destination and wheeled round, landing heavily on the rooftop. He fought for a moment against a strong gust of wind, adjusting his hold on the apex of the roof, powerful claws scarring the soft lead flashing as he did so.

Finding a sheltered spot between two chimneys Mordecai set to work unpicking the leather thong that tied the cylindrical package across his chest. His sharp beak picked deftly at the knotted leather, but the hide had stretched and tightened in the rain and he could not undo it. Thunder cracked overhead and a bolt of electricity shot down one of the dozen lightning rods that punctuated the roofs of the great house. Mordecai jumped at the spark of flame as it flashed past him.

With renewed energy he plucked at the stubborn knot, but it would not budge. Finally he snapped at the leather strap, his razor sharp beak slicing through the bonds as easily as cutting through butter. The package dropped, hitting the roof and rolling quickly down the steeply-sloping tiles. Mordecai squawked, chasing the runaway parcel down the gable, his claws scraping and sliding on the wet tiles. With a supreme effort, he lunged forwards and managed to catch the cylinder in his beak, holding it fast as he fought his way back up the roof and onto the chimney top. There, with one final effort he finally loosened his grip on his cargo, letting the parcel drop into the well of the chimney beneath him.

His mechanical eye watched for a moment as it descended into the darkness below. Then, his task completed, he lifted his strong black and white wings and rose up into the angry sky, following a course back to his master.

*

"Oh, what's taking all the time?" Dotty asked Geoff. "Surely Skitter must have told them where the Vagabond King's hideout is by now." She impatiently kicked a cushion across the room. "I want to go and fetch Joe." She scowled at the rain spitting rudely against her bedroom window. She was paced up and down the room. She had been sitting in her habitual spot in the window trying to read, but with all the waiting she was beginning to feel a bit stir-crazy and her mind kept wondering. The waiting was killing her. Geoff let out a bored whine, head on his paws.

She sat down again, giving the book another go. But it was no use. Her eyes strayed outside to the rain-battered glasshouses in the distance. Dotty groaned. Some fresh air would have helped, of course, but the weather was clearly against her. Putting the book down once more beside her, she sulkily swung her legs down from the cushioned window seat.

"It's no use Geoff, I just can't wait any longer. Let's go and see if Great Uncle Winchester has any news yet."

Geoff pricked his ears up at the mention of his master, raising his head off his paws and cocking his head on one side.

"Hmm," she said, thinking. "I think we'll rollerblade it, shall we? It's quicker."

Geoff made a distorted expression and, exhaling loudly, slumped back down onto his paws. Dotty knew that he hated rollerblading. He was afraid of their vicious little wheels narrowly avoiding him – well, most of the time. Dotty, meanwhile, continued to gather enthusiasm for the idea.

"Yes, I definitely think that would be quickest. And if he hasn't heard anything yet we can go exploring around some of the house that I haven't seen yet; there's always loads of cool stuff to discover. Remember the other day we found that room full of blown eggs?"

Geoff turned his head, making a show of ignoring her.

"And then when we've finished perhaps we can take a trip down to the kitchen?" Dotty strode across the room, unhooking her rollerblades from the back of the bedroom door. She eyed her dog slyly. "Maybe a spot of hot chocolate," she continued, "and whatever Gobby has baking in the kitchen?"

The promise of food was all the greedy spaniel had needed. He got to his feet and barked in agreement to the plan, tail wagging in anticipation.

"That's my boy," said Dotty, giving his head an affectionate rub. She began to tie her skates.

But she never finished. A sudden crack of thunder made her jump. Then, a split second later, lightning shot down the metal conductor that ran down the roof just outside Dotty's bedroom window, leaving a prickle of electricity in the room as it passed by. "Phew! That was a close one," she remarked, before being distracted by another noise: the clatter of something falling down the chimney.

Geoff barked. Dotty stood up, skating across the room, laces askew. "Do you think the lightning dislodged a brick or something?" she asked the dog.

Gingerly, she poked her head up into the open flue, fearful of falling rubble; but the only thing that fell on her upturned face was icy spots of rain. Geoff barked again. "Yes, yes, I'll be careful," she replied. She squinted upwards. There was definitely something wedged just above head height: it didn't look like a brick though.

"Pip?" she called out, suddenly suspecting something more than the storm was responsible for the unexpected arrival. No answer. Geoff tugged at her jumper, warning her against whatever was stuck in the chimney. She pushed him away gently and reached up carefully to dislodge the object. A sudden rush of soot made Dotty jump back as it landed with a *thwump* in the fire grate. The foreign object nestled in amongst it. Gingerly, Dotty fished it out. It was a package, an old-fashioned cylindrical document holder, tied with a leather thong.

The Delivery

Chapter 14

Hearths and Homes

In which Dotty talks rescue with Great Uncle Winchester and the cook becomes a nursemaid

"Dear Dorothy," the letter read.

"Some information has come my way that I believe may serve both of us well. I hear you are in possession of a certain locket of power for which I have been searching. I myself am in possession of a certain boy for whom I understand you have been searching. My terms are simple. Give me the locket and I will bring you Joe. Be ready with your answer at sundown.

The Vagabond King "

Dotty's head spun, first with relief from the confirmation that Joe was alive and okay, but then with a terrible sense of guilt. Was she really the reason that Joe had been taken? Surely that could not be what this was all about? She couldn't quite believe it. Suddenly she wished she had never found her mother's locket; that it had remained hidden up the chimney for another thirty years. But then, how was she to know it was magical? Or that it would be the cause of all this trouble?

She needed to speak to Great Uncle Winchester straight away. To tell him she had a way of rescuing Joe, although it would mean giving up the Calendar House Key. It was a high price to pay, but worth it. If only they had found Sarah earlier. Skitter could have given them Joe's whereabouts and none of this would be necessary. Still, there was no point crying over spilt milk, Dotty thought. They were going to get Joe back and that was all that mattered right now.

She hurtled down the corridor. "Great Uncle Winchester! Winnie, you've got to see this." She was in such a hurry that she fell over her skates and made the last part of the journey down the panelled hallway in a momentous skid that left her in an untidy pile at her uncle's study door.

"My dear girl, whatever is it?" Great-Uncle Winchester appeared in the doorway, a half-eaten corned beef sandwich still protruding from his mouth, greasy breadcrumbs stuck in his enormous sideburns.

Dotty untangled herself as best she could, struggling to her feet. Her great uncle's attire was distinctly maritime today. As if he was going sailing, Dotty thought, or at least considering it.

Catching her breath, Dotty held out the leather cylinder and was about to explain its contents when her great-uncle grabbed it out of her hands, with an almighty "Arr-harrrrgh!" First he put it to his eye as if it were a telescope, then he waved it around dramatically as if it were a sword, but finally he pulled off the lid.

"What have we here, Mistress Dorothea?" he asked her playfully. "Methinks it might be a treasure map, showing the hidden location of a hoard of pirate gold, eh?" He took the paper out of its casing and waved it about. "What say you, dear girl? Does 'X' mark the spot?" He put a hand on his hip, striking a jaunty sailor pose.

Usually Dotty would have loved her great uncle's playfulness. She adored his childish antics and was at all other times game for any adventure that his vivid imagination conjured up. But as her mam would have said, 'now was not the time or the place'.

"Why are you in such a good mood, anyway?" she asked.

"My dear, now that the girl, Sarah, is safe, we have been able to coax out of our captive an address: the location, no less, of the lair of the

Vagabond King." The old man looked very pleased with himself. "I am quietly confident that the scouts will find your friend Joe and bring him back to us this very night."

"Wow," exclaimed Dotty. "Well that's definitely a good reason to celebrate. We might not even need to meet with him after all."

"Meet with Joe, dear girl?"

"No, with the Vagabond King. He wants to do an exchange: to give up Joe in exchange for the Calendar House Key. It's all in the letter," Dotty gestured at the leather package, now lying redundant in her great uncle's hand.

"Well that is interesting news," replied her uncle, sitting down to read the note. Dotty sat down quietly opposite him, waiting for him to finish reading.

"It is hoped we won't need to make use of this offer, but I think we must still set up the meeting."

"But why? From what you've said we will have Joe by then and it won't be necessary."

"Yes, my dear, but we have to prepare for every eventuality. There is still a chance the scouts might not find Joe. And besides, if we do not agree to meet with him he will be suspicious, and we cannot risk that."

Suddenly Dotty felt less than sure that her friend would be rescued.

"But what if the scouts don't find Joe? What happens then?"

"Oh, my dear girl," he sighed. "Then I think you would have a decision to make, would you not?"

Dotty found it almost as unbearable to think of giving up the Calendar House Key as it was to consider the possibility of not getting Joe back. "What are we going to do?" she asked.

Winnie sat back in his chair, the paper still in one hand, pinching the bridge of his nose with the other. He closed his eyes for a moment, as if deep in thought.

"Winnie?" Dotty prompted.

"Well, my dear," her great uncle answered with a sigh. "I have to say, that is really a question only you can answer, is it not?"

Dotty was confused. "Me?" she asked. "But how can it be *my* decision? This is your decision; the Council's. You told them I would keep the locket safe, that I was capable. How would it be if I were to give it away to this villain, the Vagabond King, in return for a boy? And a boy who means nothing to them," she said, tears springing to her eyes.

"But, my darling girl," Dotty's great uncle replied, leaning forward in his chair, giving her arm a gentle squeeze. "Joe means a great deal to you, doesn't he?"

Tears began to roll down Dotty's face. "Yes," she admitted. "Yes, he's my friend." She hadn't really put two and two together until now. But the loss of her family, her home, and now a friend who was part of the life that had been taken from her had been an almost unbearable weight to bear. She sobbed. She had to save him.

"So," the old man continued. "I think we have our answer, don't we?"

"But I can't," Dotty protested weakly. "I mean, the locket: the key. I can't let it get into the hands of the Vagabond King, surely?"

Great Uncle Winchester gently took her hand. "Dorothea, remember there is a good chance it may not even come to that. With luck my scouts will return with Joe any time now, and the exchange will not be necessary."

"Your scouts?"

"The Council's, of course," Dotty's great uncle corrected his slip. "If not, then we must go through with the exchange," he said firmly. "We will deal with the consequences when they arise. It's as simple as that."

Dotty was dumfounded. She had been so sure that her great uncle was going to say they would have to find another way, even though with every fibre in her body she had hoped that he would agree to the Vagabond King's demands. To have to give up the Key, after all they had been through to keep it from the hands of the sweep traders only a few months before, seemed a bitter pill to swallow, even to Dotty. So she was relieved but shocked that he had so readily agreed.

But if the scouts weren't able to bring Joe back, for whatever reason, it would buy his freedom, and that was what they had to focus on for now. Dotty stood to go, feeling a bit shaky. She forgot she was still wearing her skates and almost lost her legs from under her, but her great uncle took her by the elbow, enabling her to recover her feet before she lost them.

"You know," he said, slowly releasing her arm and letting her stand alone. "In my experience these things have a habit of working themselves out. You'll see."

Then all of a sudden he was back to his usual playful self. "So, mistress, I say we send a message across our bows to this Vagabond King and his band of scurvy thieves and arrange a pirate's parlay without delay." He presented her with the leather cylinder, waving it in the air in a curly motion as he bowed deeply to her. "Milady," he said.

Dotty smiled, despite herself. "Aye, aye, cap'n," she replied.

"Now be off with you and find that dratted housekeeper of mine," said her great uncle, coming out of character again. "I swear the woman's spending far too long with that child. Mutinous behaviour, if you ask me."

What Great Uncle Winchester had said was true. The nursery seemed to have become Gobby's new home since their house guest had arrived. As they had strayed onto the subject,

Dotty took the opportunity to ask a question that had been bothering her since they had rescued Skitter's sister from the Tanneries.

"Winnie, the little girl: Sarah. She seemed very ill when we found her."

Dotty's great uncle was serious again for a moment. "Yes, my dear, I fear she is."

"Then why is she here? Why hasn't she been taken to the hospital?" she asked.

"Alas, dear girl," he replied. "However would we explain her? She has no records, no presence in the outside world. On paper at least, beyond the walls of this house, she simply doesn't exist." Great Uncle Winchester smiled a small sad smile at his great niece before resuming a playful air.

"Now off you go, me hearty, and when you see my housekeeper won't you tell her she forgot my pudding!" he shouted after Dotty as she skated back up the corridor towards the nursery.

*

The nursery was not one room, but a suite of rooms at the top of the house of which her mother's playroom was just one. Under normal circumstances the other rooms were out of use; the bedrooms, bathroom, dressing rooms, and school room all being kept under the protective cover of numerous dust sheets, as Mam's playroom had been when Dotty discovered it. But now Skitter's sister, Sarah, was there. And so the blinds in these long forgotten rooms had been drawn back, the windows opened to let in just the right amount of fresh air, the dust sheets drawn back and the bedding aired. The result was a series of bright, airy spaces under the eaves of the great house: a happy space for any number of small children to live and play. But, with the exception of Mam's playroom, which Dotty still frequented on a regular basis, the rooms had only a single occupant.

Sarah was staying in the nursery bedroom farthest from the playroom. As Dotty neared the room, she felt the air of hushed silence that surrounded it and instinctively slowed her approach. Stopping for a moment to remove her rollerblades, she tiptoed noiselessly along the nursery corridor and waited patiently at the door to be let in.

Standing in the doorway, Dotty watched for a moment as Gobby busied herself around the room, moving silently in stockinged feet, stoking the fire and smoothing the bedsheets around their motionless guest. Gobby spied Dotty and signalled to her to come in. The room was darkened by the blinds, which were half drawn. A shaft of sunlight filtered across to the bed. It was stiflingly warm on account of the fire blazing on such a mild day, but Gobby insisted on keeping it on, for fear that a chill might bring further harm to the patient. There was a breeze near the window that eased it slightly, at least, playing with the nets through the gap in the curtains. Sarah was asleep.

"Come in, dear," Gobby instructed quietly, dipping a clean white cloth in a bowl at the bedside and mopping the little girl's forehead. "She's very weak. No appetite—she eats like a bird." Gobby shook her head sadly. "I fear we are going to lose her."

Gobby perched for a moment on a dainty chair by the bed that looked too small and delicate to support her weight, the chair almost disappearing beneath her skirts as she sat. "I know Mr Winchester said she'd already been to the hospital, and that they can't do any more for her, but I do think we should get a second opinion. Call a doctor out or something." She hesitated, adding, "If only she wasn't so weak..."

Dotty had never heard Gobby speak out against Great Uncle Winchester before. But she understood her frustration and had shared it until her conversation with her great uncle only a moment before. Gobby looked so sad. For a moment the old woman looked almost as frail as the little girl who lay still under the pretty patchwork quilt that covered the bed. Dotty's heart went out to the old cook.

"Is there anything I can do, Mrs Gobbins?" Dotty asked. "Shall I sit with her for a while?"

"No, it's all right, dear, thank you for asking," replied Gobby. "I want to keep an eye on her myself. Do sit with me for a while, though," she added. "Keep an old woman company."

Dotty obliged her, sitting cross-legged on the floor near Gobby's chair.

"What's wrong with her, anyway? Is it her legs?" Dotty asked, remembering the steel calipers that encircled the little girl's legs.

"Oh no, my dear, that's the rickets. Not something we see very often nowadays hereabouts. It's caused by a poor diet. This little urchin has been starved since the day she was born, by the looks of it." Gobby let out a sigh. "It's the pneumonia that's doing for her. She just hasn't the strength to shift it. Where did Mr Winchester say that he found her? In Leeds? My, he's a one for taking in strays," she complained, but Dotty could hear an edge of pride in her voice. She thought highly of her master's kindness. "I say, I hope he cleared it with the authorities. Don't know what kind of trouble we might get into if she has family out there somewhere, looking for her."

"She has a brother," Dotty replied, keen to stem this particular strain of questioning quickly. "Great-Uncle Winchester is looking for him, I think."

"Oh, well that's happy news," said Gobby, but her voice cracked as she spoke and she had to stop to wipe a tear from the corner of her eye. "I just hope Mr Winchester can find him in time."

Dotty gave the old woman a hug. "Don't worry," she said reassuringly. "She'll be okay."

Dotty looked at Sarah. Her breathing was shallow, her skin pale and waxy. Beads of sweat clung to her forehead, sticking strands of her dark hair to her face. Her eyelids fluttered as she slept. Dotty hoped she was dreaming of something nice, but she feared that was not the case. Whatever had she been through before Pip and Dotty had found her in the Tanneries? Dotty couldn't bear to think.

"I almost forgot," Dotty said, recalling her uncle's last words as she had left him a little while before. "Great-Uncle Winchester says you didn't send his pudding."

"Pudding!" the cook roared. "Asking for pudding when there's a little girl dying under his roof? That man thinks about nothing but his stomach. I'll give him pudding."

Dotty was pleased to see the return of the feisty cook she knew and loved.

"You can tell him to go and help himself to a slice of treacle tart from shelf in the larder. Or there's some cake in the tin."

Dotty smiled. "Yes, Mrs Gobbins."

"Tell him he knows where it is, he goes in there enough when he thinks I'm not looking."

Dotty giggled.

"I swear that man's as bad as his dog!" Gobby muttered. Dotty thought that she was probably right. Neither one of them could see further than their own stomachs for the majority of the time.

"Okay, I'll tell him," said Dotty. Then in a hushed tone, she asked, "Mrs Gobbins, do you really think we're going to lose her. Sarah, I mean?"

Gobby sighed a big sigh. "I don't know, dear," she admitted. "By rights she should be fine now, but if the will isn't there... It's like she's pining for something; for her parents, maybe, or this brother of hers." She smoothed her skirts thoughtfully. "Perhaps when your great-uncle finds him she will perk up. We have to hope. If not, well, I'm flummoxed."

Gobby paused. "I really do think we should call a doctor in, even if it's just for a second opinion. Do you know, now I come to think of it I'm going to go downstairs and mention it to your Mr Winchester again," she resolved. "And I suppose I might as well get him his pudding whilst I'm there," she huffed.

"Okay, Mrs Gobbins." Dotty didn't envy her great uncle having to explain that one away. "In that case, I'll just sit here with Sarah for a few minutes, if you don't mind."

"Yes of course, dear. I'm sure she'd like that."

So as Gobby bustled off down the corridor, Dotty sat down at Sarah's bedside and took up the old woman's vigil.

Dotty watched as Sarah slept. Or was she unconscious? Dotty couldn't be sure.

"Sarah, are you awake?" she asked quietly. But the little girl didn't respond. Dotty took her hand. It was so cold, despite the heat in the room. She gave Sarah's hand a squeeze, willing her to react, to give it a little squeeze back – to show that she still had some fight left in her, but she remained quite still.

"This should never have happened to you," Dotty told her, bitterly. "I wish there was something I could do to make you well again."

Sarah's eyes flickered a reply, her mouth showing the faintest glimmer of a smile. Dotty imagined the girls' hand twitching a response, although in truth she was so weak it was hard to tell.

As she sat there Dotty's mind turned to the Vagabond King's letter. It had said that the Vagabond King would send for an answer to his proposal that evening, and Dotty sat on Sarah's bed wondering exactly what that meant. Should she write another note and put it in the leather document holder? Would it be magically whisked back up the chimney somehow? Or would a messenger appear to take it? Or worse, would the King himself come to demand his answer?

She eyed the nursery fireplace nervously, almost expecting someone to appear at any moment. But there was no movement from the chimney. Instead, just her mind turned back to the little girl beside her, there came a tapping at the window pane.

Tap, tap, tap. She had heard that noise before and it gave her the shivers. She thought of the jackdaws, the unwelcome spies of evil sweep traders Porguss and Poachling, who had broken into the house when they were trying to steal the Calendar House Key. Yes, now she came to think of it, it made sense that the Vagabond King would send one of those horrible birds to do his dirty work for him. Trembling, she drew the blind back from the window. Dotty screamed.

"Have ye an answer for the King?" the bird croaked through the glass.

The giant magpie was the single largest bird Dotty had ever seen, his huge frame filling the entire window, great claws clinging to the window ledge, scarring the woodwork with razor-sharp talons. Some kind of camera appeared to be strapped to its head with thick brown leather straps. The camera lens moved, whirring loudly as it zoomed in and out, a red light shining in her face, blinding her. Dotty shaded her eyes to better look at the terrifying messenger. She could see now that the camera was in place of one of the bird's eyes. It was like something out of a sci-fi movie, or the most vivid of nightmares.

"Yes," Dotty whispered, barely speaking. Then more loudly, "Yes, I do."

"Ye will hand over the Key, then?" it asked, its voice rasping beyond the glass.

"I will," replied Dotty.

"Very well," said the bird. "The King'll meet ye in the Tanneries three days hence at sundown, on the corner of Three Street and Hangman's Row. Do not be late." The terrible eye focused in on her. "And come alone."

Their exchange over, the bird flapped its great wings, lifting itself up into the sky and across the rooftops of the Calendar House.

Dotty watched as the messenger flew away into the distance. Suddenly she felt desperate to speak to someone – to see a familiar face. She gave Sarah's hand a final squeeze. "I'm going to speak to Sylv," she whispered. "See you later." Then quietly she padded out of the room.

Back in her bedroom, Dotty slumped down on her bed, iPad in hand, and jabbed at the Skype button. Sylv came flickering into view. The Wi-Fi signal wasn't great at the house. Sylv was wearing her favourite onesie: pink and furry with bunny rabbit ears. Dotty thought she looked like an overgrown stuffed toy in it, but she didn't dare say so. Things had been a bit awkward ever since Dotty had teased Sylv over Pip, and she didn't want to make any more waves right now.

"Hiya, Dot," Sylv drawled in her thick South Wales accent. She was busy painting her short, bitten nails in a lurid glitter pink, presumably to match the onesie. "What d'you reckon?"

Dotty shuddered. Sometimes she really had no idea how they had come to be best friends.

"I've got news," said Dotty, "about Joe; quite a bit of news, actually."

Sylv abandoned the nail painting and sat up on her bed, pulling herself closer to the screen. "What news? Is it good?" she asked nervously.

"Sort of, well, yes," replied Dotty. "We know where the Vagabond King's lair is, and the Council have sent scouts out to find it. Hopefully they'll be bringing Joe home any time soon."

"But that's brilliant, isn't it?"

"Great Uncle Winchester seems pretty confident about it, yes. And there's more," continued Dotty. "We've had a letter too."

"Who from?"

"The Vagabond King."

Dotty explained about the strange package that had come down her chimney and the Vagabond King's offer to return Joe in exchange for the Calendar House Key.

"But what does he want your mam's locket for?" Sylv asked.

"I don't know. Great Uncle Winchester said it has something to do with his master plan: to stop the 'ordinary folk', as they call us, from entering the world of sweeps. Apparently he doesn't think we're worthy of their attention; wants to separate the two worlds forever. It's all pretty creepy, if you ask me."

"Creepy doesn't cover it, Dot. The man's completely *twp*[2]," Sylv stared at the screen, wide-eyed. "But, 'ang on a minute, Dot: doesn't that mean no more chimney hopping, like? I mean, you'd 'ave to get the train down for the weekend, and...and there'd be no more Pip." Sylv looked genuinely upset at the idea.

"Well, yeah, Sylv, there's that. But it's a pretty big deal for the Sweep's Council as well. After all, they entrusted the locket to me. I mean, it's pretty bad that I've only had it a few months and I'm going to have to give it away to their arch enemy."

Sylv bit a nail.

"He says he wants to make the exchange on Friday at sundown: the Key for Joe. That's only three days away, Sylv."

"Well he's going to be too late, isn't he? I mean, the Council's scouts will have already brought him home by then."

"I hope so. But we're going to agree to the exchange in case they can't pull it off. I don't know, Sylv. Even though I know it's just a back-up plan, just the thought of agreeing to give up the Key gives me a really bad feeling."

Suddenly, from inside the house there came an almighty shriek, making Dotty jump with fright. It was Gobby.

---

[2] Welsh for 'stupid' or 'mad'.

"My kitchen." she hollered. "The fireplaces. My ovens are gone!"

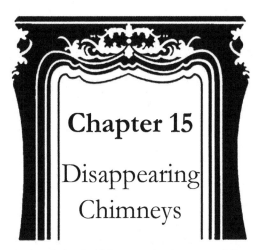

Chapter 15

Disappearing Chimneys

In which the Calendar House is laid siege and Dotty has a visit from a faerie.

Dotty scrambled down the back stairs and into the kitchen. Gobby was right – the kitchen ranges were all missing. Where once the polished stoves sat nestled in the huge chimney breasts in all four corners of the room, there was just a continuation of the brown walls that had surrounded them. It was as if they had simply never been there. Dotty blinked and blinked again, struggling to believe her eyes, but no amount of looking would restore the cast iron ranges or bright copper kettles that had stood upon them.

Gobby was distraught. The poor woman stood in the centre of the room gaping and turning, first one way then another. Her mouth opened and shut but for the most part no words came out, giving her the appearance of a fish out of water, gasping for air. Dotty had never seen her like this before and she was quite worried the poor woman might actually lose her mind at the thought of having no way of baking for the master of the house.

Dotty considered suggesting the woman make a salad, but, "I'll go and fetch Great Uncle Winchester," in the end was all the reassurance Dotty could muster.

Not for the first time that day, she raced along the corridor, shouting at the top of her lungs. "Winnie, the ovens have gone!" Dotty was met at the study door by Geoff, who barked a greeting, but Dotty ignored the dog, walking straight past him and into the empty study. Her great-uncle wasn't there.

"Oh gosh!" exclaimed Dotty. "He was here a moment ago." Now she had to think what to do. Should she call Pip? Or tend to the hysterical cook first? "I'm too young for all this responsibility, you know!" she shouted to the walls. Right, think, think, *think*, Dotty. What to do next? She would have to draft in help. Dotty hurtled back down the corridor, through the kitchen where Gobby was still rooted to the spot, down the service corridor, past the butler's room, the pantry, the laundry, the boot room and the game larder, and out in to the garden. "Kenny," she called "Where are you?"

The old gardener appeared from between the cabbages, a concerned look on his face. "What is it, Miss Dotty? Are you quite all right?"

"Yes I'm fine, but Mrs Gobbins isn't. Somebody seems to have played a, er, trick on her."

"A trick, you say?"

"Yes, Kenny. You need to come and have a look." Dotty pulled him by the cuff, urging him to come.

The gardener dropped his rake and followed Dotty back into the house.

It was a gamble. At first, Dotty thought that she was going to be left with two hysterical old folk in the kitchen, but after a moment of shocked silence, Kenny set to work, ushering Gobby into her fireside chair (although it no longer had a fire to sit next to) and, producing his hip flask, poured her a large slug of brandy into a teacup which she gratefully accepted.

With Kenny in charge of Gobby, Dotty set off to call Pip, running to the nearest room with a fireplace intact, which was the Bird Room (so called by Dotty because of the fanciful birds that adorned the wallpaper). She had more or less avoided this room since her near-capture there a few months ago at the hands of Porguss and Poachling. She still felt uneasy entering the pretty sitting room that had, prior to the incident, been her favourite of the formal rooms in the house.

Scanning the dainty drawing room with her eyes, she noticed that the glass in the glass house, smashed by thousands of jackdaws crashing through the French windows on the night of her attack, hadn't been mended yet. They stood boarded up, partly obscured by the blinds that covered them.

The Bird Room was a lot darker without the light flooding in through the glass house, and Dotty couldn't help peering suspiciously into all the dark corners as she crossed the room to the fireplace. Grabbing the bell-pull, she yanked on it firmly, knowing that it would signal Pip— although she didn't hear any ringing for her efforts. Pip mustn't have been far away, however, because he appeared almost at once, looking rather surprised at the place Dotty had chosen to call him from.

"Emergency," she explained. "The kitchen ranges have all gone missing."

Pip looked grave. "This is what I've been telling you about," he said, shaking his head in dismay. "It's the Vagabond King. There are more every day now. Soon, there won't be any flues left for us to travel." He sat down on the sofa, smearing the cream brocade with soot and looking for the world as if he was carrying the weight of it upon his shoulders.

Dotty suddenly felt very guilty for not having really paid attention to Pip's reports about the disappearances before. She had been so focused on finding Joe that in truth she hadn't been interested in what he had to say. And, to be honest, a few disappearing chimneys hadn't seemed important in comparison to her vanished friend. The real significance of the situation was starting to hit home now, though, and Dotty felt wretched along with Pip.

"What we need," said Dotty in a chirpy voice, trying to be positive, "is a way to stop the disappearances."

"What we need," replied Pip miserably, "is some sort of miracle."

As if in answer to their prayers, at that very moment there was a rustle in the grate, and Dotty and Pip turned round. She saw a small brown creature dusting itself off, having obviously just followed Pip down the chimney.

Pip grabbed the creature at once, "Don't worry, It's just a hob," he said, which explained nothing to Dotty. "I'll get rid of it. Strange though, they don't usually stray too far from the kitchen hearth." He waved the creature about in his fist as he spoke.

"Might be something to do with the fact that there *is* no kitchen hearth," quipped Dotty.

"Ouch! It bit me," Pip dropped the creature on the floor. It sat up and rubbed itself, obviously sore from its tumble. Then, drawing itself up to its full height, which wasn't much, it fixed a disapproving eye on Pip, quickly fiddling with something in its hands and then blowing hard in Pip's direction.

It was clearly some sort of magic. The effects were immediate, and like nothing else Dotty had ever seen. The creature seemed to have trapped Pip inside some kind of invisible box, although if it were made of plastic or glass, Dotty could not see it. Suddenly, the tiny being seemed to Dotty to hold more menace than Pip had given it credit for. It scared her. Pip seemed more infuriated than afraid, and banged on the hidden walls with his fists, using some fairly strong language that Dotty couldn't hear on account of the invisible box, which appeared to be sound-proof, as well as Pip-proof.

"You sweeps have always underestimated the hob folk," it said in an angry, high-pitched voice. "Unless you want something from us, of course." It turned to Dotty, who was now staring at the creature, bug-eyed. "And you must be the cause of all the trouble: Joe's friend."

Dotty gasped. This creature knew Joe? But how? "You've seen Joe?" she asked, realising as she looked at it just how ugly the little creature was: like a shrivelled old prune with a big nose and a wicked glint in its eye.

"Smart boy, that," replied the creature, making a grimace that Dotty assumed was its approximation of a smile. "I am minded to like that one. Wasted in the realm of the ordinary folk, of course," it mused.

The creature had a singsong voice and Dotty almost felt like she was listening to it talking in rhyme—as if its voice itself was an enchantment.

Dotty shook her head instinctively, as if to rid her mind of the hob's presence. "Please," she begged. "Can you tell us how to find him?"

"Joe has asked me to deliver a message to you, Miss Dotty," it replied, with a voice like the jangle of bells.

"What message?" Dotty asked. The creature seemed particularly adept at never answering a question directly, and she quickly came to the conclusion that this was a rather slippery character with whom she was dealing. She didn't trust it one bit.

It continued in the same melodic tone.

"The answer you seek lies before your blind eyes
As the hearths that are gone tell you nothing but lies.
But beware: when the King returns that which is mine
All the lies will ring true and you'll be out of time."

"What does that mean? Do you know where Joe is?" Dotty begged, desperately.

"Joe didn't ask me to tell you that," replied the hob smartly, and in a puff of brown smoke it disappeared.

"Wait!" Dotty shouted. "Come back! You never told me if Joe was all..." she faltered, "...right." It was no use; the hob was gone.

Its disappearance seemed to release Pip from his invisible prison, and he fell to the floor, panting, as if the invisible box had been short of air as well as space.

"What on earth was that?" Dotty demanded, putting out a hand to pull Pip up off the carpet. He stood, wheezing, catching his breath.

"That," he said, panting, "was a hob."

"So you said. But what is one of those?".

"Hobs are very powerful faeries. They use ancient magick, much more powerful than ours. My guess is that the Vagabond King has been using them to close the fireplaces, just like the Council thought." Pip sounded puzzled. "But why a hob would be working in league with the likes of the Vagabond King I really don't know. What did it say?" he asked. "I couldn't hear a thing."

"Not a lot that made any sense," Dotty replied. "Except that it knew Joe. It said that Joe had sent it with a message – for me. Seems everyone wants to speak to me at the moment," she said, sighing heavily.

"Okay. Well as long as it didn't try to strike a bargain with you, that's all that matters," said Pip.

"Why not strike a bargain?" Dotty asked.

"It didn't, did it?" Pip looked alarmed. "Ask for anything in return for this message, that is? Hobs are notorious for making bad bargains with people. Tricky creatures, faeries." He shook his head. "The bargains never end well for those who make them."

"Oh dear," said Dotty. "No, it didn't ask for anything,"

"Good. So what was the message?"

"It was a riddle, I suppose. I'm not sure I can remember it all."

"Try," urged Pip impatiently. "It could be important."

"Okay, okay, just a minute," Dotty moaned. "I think it was: *The answer you seek lies before your blind eyes, as the hearths that are gone tell you nothing but lies. But beware: when the King returns that which is mine, all the lies will ring true and you'll be out of time.'* Weird, huh?"

"Ugh! I hate riddles!" Pip groaned. "I hate faeries and their gobbledygook language—hey, are you all right?" He eyed Dotty with concern.

"Yeah, I'm fine. But if faeries are as bad as you say they are," Dotty said taking a shaky breath, "I'm wondering what bargain it made with Joe in return for delivering the message."

"Don't worry," said Pip, "I'm sure Joe will be fine too." He gave Dotty a reassuring squeeze on the arm. "I know: let's go speak to Mr Winchester. Hopefully he will be able to make some sense of all this."

"I tried to find him just before," Dotty shrugged, "but he wasn't in his study. We can try again, though. With any luck he'll be back now."

"Okay," agreed Pip. "Why don't you go and speak to him, if you can. I'm going to have a quick scout round the house; see if any other rooms have chimneys missing."

"Do you have to do that now? Can't you come with me?" asked Dotty, a bit put out at his suggestion of leaving her.

"We need to know how bad things are, Dotty. The kitchen may not be the only room affected," he said. "Look: I'll come and find you when I'm done."

"Okay, but – well, just don't be long, okay?"

Dotty set off back towards her great uncle's study. From the Bird Room, she had to walk past the kitchen in order to reach Her great uncle's office. The door to Gobby's domain was pulled to, so Dotty couldn't see inside, but the screaming appeared to have stopped. She hoped this was a good thing.

A quick survey of Great Uncle Winchester's study told Dotty that her great-uncle was still not returned from wherever he had got to, Feeling frustrated, and cross with Pip for leaving her, she retraced her steps back towards the service wing. At least she could see how Gobby was faring in the meantime.

On reaching the door, Dotty gave a gentle knock on the aged pine and walked in. Whilst the caterwauling had ceased, Gobby was nevertheless still most definitely beside herself. Kenny had obviously returned to his outdoor duties and the old cook was left wondering aimlessly between the kitchen and the pantry, clearly at a loose end. As she paced, the poor woman muttered to herself, mostly about how she was going to prepare dinner that evening, and that Mr Winchester wouldn't be happy without a hot meal.

The kitchen did seem strangely empty without its ovens, almost like it had lost its soul. Dotty's heart went out to her. She was clearly lost without a job to do.

"Mrs Gobbins," Dotty began, interrupting the cook mid-mutter. "I was wondering: do you think Sarah would like some of your special broth? You know, the one you made me when I was poorly? It always makes me feel so much better."

"Well, I'm sure she would, dear. But how am I to make it?"

"It's just that there's a little range in the nursery suite, isn't there?" Dotty continued. "You know, you sometimes make a pot of tea on it. I wondered whether it could be used to make soup."

Gobby's entire face lit up. The transformation was quite amazing: as if a light bulb had gone on insider her head. "Why, Dotty, if that isn't the most brilliant idea!" she exclaimed.

"Why ever didn't I think of that myself? Thank you, my girl." She beamed, seemingly now quite recovered from the shock of losing her kitchen ovens; for the moment, anyway.

"Oh, my dear, but look at the time! I'd better get started straight away." She grabbed a startled Dotty by the cheeks and gave her a great big kiss, then waddled off into the scullery to prepare the vegetables, humming as she went.

Left alone in the kitchen, Dotty waited for Pip to meet her, as promised, with a report on the state of the other chimneys in the house. Suddenly cold, she hugged herself, noticing that, without the heat of the fireplaces to warm the room, her breath was visible in the chill air. The silence was disconcerting, too. Without the sound of Gobby puffing and blowing, pans spitting and bubbling, pots scraping against each other, and the furnaces roaring, it was eerily quiet in the now useless kitchen. It gave Dotty the willies. But Pip wasn't long in returning.

"It's bad news, I'm afraid," he puffed, He had clearly been running. "Things are moving a lot more quickly than we had thought. Almost every chimney in the house has gone! I just don't know what we're going to do."

"Oh, Pip. I'm sorry," said Dotty. "But I'm sure we'll find a way around this – you'll see."

"We'd better," he said grimly. "Soon there won't be any chimneys left, and when you give up the Calendar House Key to the Vagabond King, that will put pay to ordinary folk travelling between our world and yours, too. We'll be separated forever."

"But there will still be Great-Uncle Winchester's window, won't there?" asked Dotty. "I mean, that's not a chimney. Surely that won't disappear."

"I really don't know, Miss Dotty," he replied. "Who knows where it will all end? Perhaps the Vagabond King will magic away the window, too."

Dotty stood silently for a moment, thinking. Pip shifted his weight onto one foot, leaning idly against the now blank kitchen wall.

Dotty screamed.

"Pip! Pip, where are you?" He had disappeared.

Disappearing Chimneys

Chapter 16
The Glamour

*In which Dotty and Pip discover that the missing
fireplaces are not all that they seem*

Dotty ran to the wall against which Pip had been leaning. It felt solid enough. She took a step back, heart in her stomach. She really didn't think she could cope with another disappearance. "Pip!" she cried.

Seconds passed, but it felt like a lifetime. Her heart raced out of control. But then she began to hear laughter. Could that be him?

"If this is some kind of joke, it really isn't funny," she shouted.

The chuckling continued as Pip stepped back out of the wall. Dotty gasped and then hit him, more than once.

"Ow, ouch! Dotty, stop!" complained Pip.

"What are you doing, walking in and out of walls?" Dotty wailed, tears of relief springing to her eyes. She had been so afraid that he was gone, too. "Were you trying to scare me half to death? I suppose you're going to tell me you're a ghost now, too, are you?"

"No, miss, I'm flesh and blood, just like you—as you well know 'cause you've just been pounding on me for the last minute." He rubbed a sore arm.

"Oh, so it was a practical joke then." Dotty accused.

"No, I swear! It wasn't me! It's the fireplaces: they're not really gone! Look, see?" He passed his hand in and out of the wall. "The fireplaces are still there. It's just a glamour: an illusion, you see?"

"Will you stop doing that, you're making me queasy?" moaned Dotty. "And what do you mean, it's a glamour? I wish you'd speak English sometimes." her relief was quickly giving way to annoyance.

"It's the hob, don't you see? That tricksy fairy has made a fool of the Vagabond King! Tell me the start of that riddle again. Go on," he instructed.

"Okay," she hesitated, "but you've still got a lot of explaining to do, as far as I'm concerned." Dotty cleared her throat and recited in a droning voice, *"The answer you seek lies before your blind eyes, as the hearths that are gone tell you nothing but lies"*.

"So the fireplaces are lying to us, right? But how?"

"A glamour is a faerie's trick," Pip explained. "The oldest in the book," he grinned, clearly delighted with the discovery.

"But I touched the wall and it felt solid enough to me. If it's not real, how come you can pass through it and I can't?"

"It's a trick of the senses. A glamour can fool your eyes, ears, nose, touch—taste even. To you ordinary folk, a faerie could make a mud pie taste like Mrs Gobbins' best lemon meringue: you see?"

"I guess so. But why doesn't it work on you?" Dotty asked.

"Well, it does, to a point, but we sweeps are magical beings, so we aren't quite as susceptible to it as you ordinary folk are." He paused. "I didn't see the glamour either at first, but when I put my hand on it well, let's just say I could feel the magick. And once you recognise it, you can pass through." He continued, excited, "If your senses don't recognize it, it'll feel as strong as bricks and mortar – like it does to you. Anyway, the how isn't important; it's that we know about it what counts. Glamours only last for a while. The chimneys will come back. We just have to wait. I must go and tell the Council straight away. Imagine: we were thinking all our chimneys were disappearing, but it was a simple hob's curse. Ha!" he grinned.

"Okay, okay, I get it," Dotty conceded slowly, "but wait how long? I don't think we can afford to just stand around and wait for them to come back. And what about the rest of the riddle? Now we know the first bit, shouldn't we find out what the second half of it means, too? It might be important."

"You're right," Pip agreed. "What was it again?"

Dotty chanted, *"But beware: when the King returns that which is mine, all the lies will ring true and you'll be out of time."*

"That which is mine," he muttered. "That which is mine. Of course! Why didn't I think of it before? That's how the Vagabond King's been getting the faerie to help him. He's stolen its name!"

"Why does that matter?" Dotty asked.

"A faerie's name holds all its power. If the King releases its name to the four winds, the hob will be rendered powerless and all his magic will be destroyed. My, no wonder it is cross." Pip let out a long whistle.

"What did I do to get myself muddled up in all of this?" she muttered to herself. Then more clearly she added. "So the faerie's name has been stolen. But what's the bit about 'being out of time'?"

"The lies will ring true," Pip mused. *"and you'll be out of time.* Hmmm, time," he pondered. Suddenly all the blood drained from Pip's face "Oh, my gosh. Time!"

"What is it? Pip, whatever's the matter?" Dotty asked.

"If the riddle is right," he replied, "that means the hob intends to make good his promise. He's going to seal all the chimneys forever, just as soon as the Vagabond King returns its name. We have to stop him and now." He took her by the hand. "Look, we've really no time to wait for Mr Winchester. We have to tell the Council this minute. Will you come with me to the Council Chamber? We'll chimney hop. It'll be quickest."

"Sure," said Dotty, her head in a whirl. "But I can't use the chimneys here. I can't get through the glamour, can I?"

"No," replied Pip. "If your senses are fooled into thinking it's solid, you won't be able to pass. We'll have to find an open chimney."

"My bedroom was okay when I left it," said Dotty. "We could try there."

It wasn't far. The pair raced up the back stairs from the kitchen and through the first floor corridor to Dotty's bedroom. But when they got there, Dotty's heart sank. The fireplace in her bedroom had vanished.

"Oh, this is hopeless," wailed Dotty. "Now what are we going to do?"

"There's another way," Pip said. "Another entrance we can use. I've seen your great-uncle use it."

"Okay," said Dotty in relief. "Let's use it then."

Pip looked a bit shifty. "I'm not sure we should. It's secret."

Dotty huffed. "I thought you said this was an emergency? Look, we don't have time for secrets now. Let's just get there, shall we?"

Pip took a deep breath. "Okay then," he agreed. "It's in his study. Run!"

Dotty and Pip hurtled down the stairs and along the seemingly never-ending corridor. On reaching the study, Dotty knocked at the door, although she didn't really expect an answer. But this time, much to her surprise and relief, they found that Her great uncle had returned.

Pip was the first to speak. "Mr Winchester, sir, we bring news. The chimneys: they are not sealed after all. It's nothing but a glamour."

"I can't pass through them, but Pip can," Dotty chimed in.

Her great uncle nodded. "Well, that's a clever finding indeed. How did you come across it?"

"By accident," replied Pip. "But there's more," he panted. "We've had a visit from the hob what done the magick."

"The hob in question came to see you?" At once Great-Uncle Winchester looked concerned. "What did it want in return for this information?"

"It asked for nothing, Mr Winchester, Sir. But it delivered a riddle.

"Tell me."

Pip recited it. Great Uncle Winchester seemed to get its meaning instantly. "I see, so the hob is intending to demand the return of its name in exchange for making good on its promise to close the chimneys."

"Yes, I believe that's it, sir," Pip replied. "And we don't have much time. I've been checking all over the house, sir. There are hardly any chimneys left: even the kitchen ranges are gone."

"The ovens?" roared Great Uncle Winchester. "Good heavens! That will never do. How is Mrs Gobbins taking it?"

"Not well," replied Dotty. "She's a bit, er, lost, shall we say."

Her great-uncle sat down.

"As it happens I also have news." He sighed. "I'm afraid it isn't good though." He gave Dotty a kindly look, but she could see that he was weary. The old man bowed his head. "Oh, my dear girl, I wish I could give you the answer you wish for, but no, I'm afraid I cannot. The Council's scouts were too late: your friend had already been moved."

Dotty gasped. "Moved? But where?"

"We do not know," Her great uncle replied.

Dotty swooned, feeling the ground rushing up from under her. Pip caught her by the elbow and helped her to a seat.

Her great uncle continued. "All the scouts were able to report was that there were two empty cages, one much larger than the other. From what you are telling me I can only surmise that one was for Joe and the other for this hob of whom you speak. With the hob he might have thought Joe's hiding place no longer safe."

"It can't be," cried Dotty. "Now we're never going to find him." A horrible feeling of hopelessness washed over her.

"To the contrary, my dear, you will find him," replied Great-Uncle Winchester sagely. "For tomorrow evening you are going to meet the Vagabond King. And he will give your friend Joe to you in exchange for the Calendar House Key."

"He's right," said Pip. "It's the only option left. You're going to have to go back into the Tanneries."

Chapter 17

The

Exchange

In which Dotty ventures back into the Tanneries to rescue
Joe

As the Vagabond King's feathered messenger had
demanded it, Dotty was determined to meet the
King alone. Pip had tried to persuade Dotty to let
him go with her anyway, but Dotty wouldn't hear
of it: she didn't want to take any risks that might
put Joe in further danger.

Nevertheless. Pip insisted on walking Dotty
most of the way through the town to the edge of
the Tanneries, which was actually just as well.
Dotty had never had much of a sense of direction
and would have most certainly become lost if she
had been left to navigate the tangle of dark and
narrow side streets alone. And so it was that they

stopped at the entrance of the dingy side street that housed the orphanage where only days before they had sought news of Sarah.

"Okay," said Pip. "This is it. It's not far, now. You're already on Three Street. Just continue along the road until you reach the junction. You'll see the sign for Hangman's Row on your right."

Dotty took a deep breath. "All right. Straight on and then to Hangman's Row."

"That's it," Pip confirmed. He lent forward and gave her a kiss on the cheek. "Don't worry, Miss Dotty, you're going to be all right."

Dotty flushed. Had he really just kissed her? She felt pleased and embarrassed all at the same time. And, unusually for Dotty, rather shy. "Okay, thanks," she mumbled, and strode off alone up the crowded street, trying to stand tall and walk with as much confidence as possible. Her face glowed from the brush of his skin on her cheek. She was desperate to look back, but she didn't want Pip to think she was unsure about the exchange, so she resisted the urge and hurried on, keeping her eyes peeled for the sign that indicated the start of Hangman's Row.

"Don't worry," Pip called after her. "I won't be far behind you. If you get into trouble, just shout and I'll be there in a trice."

Suddenly, Dotty wished for all the world that she could take Pip with her. Of course she welcomed his reassurances but, in truth, in that moment as she walked through the tumbledown alleyway, she had never in her life felt more alone.

Pip was right; it wasn't far, although far enough that he was now firmly out of sight. The place that the Vagabond King had designated for their meeting was actually at the junction of three roads: Three Street, which she was on, along Hangman's Row and Pedlar's End, a dank little side street that seemed to lead off into nothingness. The sign for Hangman's Row stood on the right as Pip had promised: rusty white lettering standing out against black iron riveted to the bricks of a building that stood at the corner two of the streets.

There was nobody there except for an old pedlar sitting with his back against the wall, idly puffing at a clay pipe. His threadbare well-patched greatcoat was drawn high up to his chin, a faded and tattered hat pulled down well over his eyes, so that she could not see his face.

Dotty didn't like to stand too close to him. She lingered a little distance away, finding shelter from the approaching night under a ripped awning. She watched and waited as the sun began to make its descent beyond the horizon, throwing shadows across the streets. Still no one stopped at the crossroads.

Presently Dotty heard the caw of a bird above her. She looked up. Circling overhead she saw a giant black-and-white magpie. It was the very same bird that had delivered the message to her from the Vagabond King. It cawed again, Dotty fancied in signal of an all-clear to its master. The sound echoed across the darkening sky, but there was nobody else on the deserted streets to pay any heed to Dotty except the pedlar.

As she lowered her eyes back towards the ground, he stood up and Dotty recognised at once that this was not the frail old man that she had imagined him to be. He drew himself up to his full height, stretching muscular limbs that had seemed stiff from crouching for so long. As he stood, his greatcoat framed his tall, powerful body, the collar that he had previously pulled tight falling away from his face. Dotty saw his strong jaw and dark skin, and felt the menace that emanated from eyes as black as coals. The Vagabond King had been there all along.

The bird stopped its circling and flew down to the ground, settling in the alleyway beside its master. "Thank you, Mordecai," the man said, without taking his eyes from Dotty. The bird also focused on the girl, its mechanical eye whirring and clicking uncannily. In the presence of the unseemly pair it was hard for Dotty not to be afraid and she instinctively grasped at the locket that encircled her neck, laying for the moment hidden beneath her jumper.

"You brought it, then," the King noted, smiling grimly. "And I, too, have kept my part of the bargain." From beneath his coat he produced a small boy. Cowering and afraid, much thinner than Dotty had ever seen him, and far dirtier than his mother would have ever allowed, was her friend.

"Joe!" Dotty flew towards him, wanting to touch him, to hug him, to tell him that he was safe now.

But the Vagabond King put out an arm, barring her way with a heavy ebony walking cane. "Tut, tut, Miss Dorothy. Where are your manners?" he mocked her. "First, the Key," he said, beckoning with his free hand.

Dotty glared at him, irritated that he'd got her name wrong and angry that he hadn't allowed her to reassure Joe. Her friend was obviously in shock and Dotty was distressed to see the sorry state that he was in. She wanted to be strong but a tear rolled down her cheek in spite of her intentions.

"The Key," the King demanded again.

Shakily, Dotty reached up behind her, feeling under her collar for the fastening of the chain that held her mother's locket. She grasped the catch and with trembling fingers fought to undo it.

"Come on, girl," snarled the King impatiently, his hand outstretched, grasping.

Dotty struggled with the catch some more. She felt the chain slacken around her neck. It was undone.

Suddenly Dotty noticed that it was becoming quite dark. The metal of the freed locket was cold on her skin as it slid down her front. She shivered a little, catching it in her hand and rescuing it from under her jumper. The Vagabond King did not move, but looked wickedly gleeful at the sight of it. Holding it by its chain, Dotty held the locket out towards the King. The locket swung a little, the gold glinting against the last rays of sunshine as the sun fell behind the tightly-packed buildings.

"Now give me Joe," she managed to say, her voice a fierce whisper.

The Vagabond King laughed cruelly. "Ha! That you would swap the Key for this," he said, referring to Joe. He shoved the boy towards Dotty as if he were nothing. Dotty moved forwards to grab him, to save him from stumbling, but something else broke his fall. It was the same thing Dotty had seen happen to Pip just a short time ago: a sort of invisible force field holding him up, picking his feet off the floor. Dotty looked around, scanning the filthy street for the only thing she knew to be capable of this kind of magic: the hob.

The direction that the Vagabond King gave to his indignant expression conveyed the hob's location to her. It was hovering just beyond Dotty's left shoulder, working its magic from behind her. She gasped and moved away. The hob ignored her, speaking directly to the Vagabond King.

"King to your own people you might be," it chanted. "But this boy is not yours to take or keep."

"Be gone, faerie, and do not meddle in affairs that do not concern you," the King sneered.

The hob was undeterred. "I made a bargain with him. The boy belongs to me," it insisted.

Dotty gasped. "No!" she cried. "Don't."

The pair ignored her. "I am warning you, hob. Release the boy," the King snarled.

The creature gave a small wicked grin. "Alas, if I could trade the boy for the return of my name you know I would. But the bargain is made. It cannot be unmade."

"Do not toy with me, creature," the Vagabond King warned.

As the pair argued, Dotty thought quickly. What on earth could she do? At last she had an idea. "The hob's name!" she called out to the Vagabond King. "You have something of the hob's too. And I bet he doesn't want to lose it."

The Vagabond King turned to Dotty, surprised, considering her with renewed interest. "Ah yes. Of course the girl is right. I do have your name." he smiled. "Release the boy to me, hob. Or I will release your name to the four winds as I promised!"

The hob looked horrified. "You wouldn't dare!" it shrieked.

"Do you want to find out?" challenged the King.

The hob thought for a moment. The force field wavered, threatening to drop Joe. But then, "You drive a hard bargain, King," it replied, seeming to regain its composure. "Of course it is only the boy's soul in which I have an interest. What say you that in exchange for my name that you may have his body?" it asked. "Will that allow you to keep your promise?"

The Vagabond King smirked at the hob. "I like your way of thinking," he chuckled. "Yes, I believe it will."

Fumbling in his pocket, he produced a tiny wooden box and tossed it in the direction of the hob. The faerie caught it gleefully. Whatever was inside was struggling to get out.

"My name!" it cried joyously.

Dotty looked on in despair. This couldn't have been further from the outcome she'd pictured. "No!" she screamed. "You can't do that." She ran to Joe, desperate to free him, hitting the force field with all her strength, but the invisible walls kept her at bay. "I won't let you have the locket," she promised. "I'd rather break it myself!" She held the locket above her head, threatening to dash it on the ground.

But before Dotty could react, the hob opened the box. Everything happened very quickly after that. There was a bright flash of blue light, blinding Dotty. Joe fell to the ground, released from the invisible force field. At the same time, the magpie lunged forwards, grabbing at the locket from Dotty's upturned hand with its razor sharp beak.

Dotty flinched; the bird had caught her as he snatched it, leaving a deep cut in her palm. Shocked, her lip trembled. As she recovered her sight she saw Joe lying unmoving on the cobbles. She ran to pick him up off the street and the bird rose up high into the sky, triumphant, holding the Calendar House Key in its beak. The precious locket that had belonged to her mother was lost to Dotty forever.

"Good doing business with you both," said the King, smirking and giving Dotty a small bow. With a wave of his greatcoat he turned and, following his henchman, rose up into the sky. As he flew he unpieced himself like some sort of horrifying jigsaw, his body disintegrating into a flock of grey-black jackdaws that separated and flew off above the rooftops.

Dotty turned to look at the hob, now unrecognisable from the ugly little brown creature she had first met at the Calendar House. A blue glow emanated from its body, which was smoothed of wrinkles, its grotesque face replaced with something delicate, beautiful, and fierce. "Hob?" Dotty asked.

"And so you have your friend," it replied. "But promises must be kept; his soul belongs to me."

"No!" begged Dotty. "Please don't take him. He has done nothing to deserve this."

"Nothing but make a bargain with a hob," the creature replied.

"But his parents are out of their minds with worry. Please!" Dotty was desperate.

The hob paused. "Two days hence, at sunset," it began. "He has until then to say his goodbyes. After that he must come with me."

And the creature was gone.

Dotty stood in the street with Joe. He was too tired from his ordeal to speak, react or even stand, and Dotty was forced to support him to prevent him from falling. Wearily, with heart and limbs like lead, Dotty turned and began to retrace her steps back towards Pip and the Calendar House.

Chapter 18

Partings

In which Joe and Sarah say goodbye

Gobby had set a bed up in the nursery suite for Joe, so that he and Sarah now occupied the same room. With a bowl of soup inside him and a crust of freshly-baked bread, Joe quickly started to recover, and before very long he was asking to be up and about exploring the house. Gobby was firm with him, though. "You need your rest," she scolded, "plenty of time for exploring when you've got your strength up." Sadly Dotty knew that time was the one thing her friend really didn't have.

Joe had a million questions for Dotty, about chimneys and sweeps and faeries; so much so that she was having a hard time keeping up with all the answers. She was pleased that he seemed his usual chirpy self, for the moment at least, though she feared that would change as the time grew nearer for the hob to come and take him. As for Dotty, she was quite sure that if the shoe were on the other foot she would not have been anywhere near as stoic as Joe was being about the whole thing. In fact, she would have been petrified.

Desperate to find a way out of Joe's bargain, when she wasn't in the nursery with him she spent all of her time poring over books in the library, hoping to discover something; anything that could help his seemingly hopeless situation. But between the legends and the folk tales, practical advice was scant and she found nothing that would tell her how to get out of a bargain with a hob, or even if it was possible to break such an agreement at all.

She wondered if Great Uncle Winchester had anything hidden away in the depths of his study, but he had done one of his disappearing acts again, and Strake wouldn't let her anywhere near since he had caught her snooping around at his employer's desk.

Whilst Joe remained decidedly perky, the story was quite different for Sarah. Since Dotty had last seen her, she appeared even more frail, almost like the shell of a girl that had once been.

"I'm afraid she hasn't got long," Gobby confided in Dotty sadly. "Poor little mite. If only there was more that I could do for her. Mr

Winchester explained the situation to me, of course."

"He did?" Dotty was surprised that he had come clean to his housekeeper about that.

"Yes, dear. That the hospital had said there was nothing further that they could do. It's so terribly sad."

"I see," replied Dotty tersely. She didn't like Her great uncle lying to his most faithful member of staff; and she liked even less the feeling that she was somehow in on it.

"Of course if our kitchen arrangements weren't so... sparse," Gobby pulled a face, "it might have made a difference."

Poor Gobby. Dotty thought it unlikely that any amount of her home cooking could have helped, no matter how good it tasted.

It took until the second day for Joe's mood to take a turn. When Dotty entered the nursery the next morning, from the look on Joe's face she knew at once what must be coming.

"You remember what happened, then," she said. "I was worried you might have forgotten, or not taken it in. I was going to talk to you about it this morning. I was dreading it, actually."

"No need," replied Joe. "I remember everything."

"I've been trying to find a way out of this; trying so hard. Joe, I'm so sorry."

"I know," Joe told her simply. But for the first time Dotty saw the fear in his eyes. "Look. I have to go and see my parents. And Jazz. I have to say goodbye."

"Oh, Joe. I don't think you can," said Dotty. "I mean, how are you going to explain that you have to leave? Might it not be worse for them to see you, only to lose you all over again?"

"You are right," Joe acknowledged, "but I have to see them, just one more time: even if they don't see me."

"All right, I'll arrange it with Sylv. We can chimney hop to Cardiff and go from hers. Oh no..." Dotty stopped as the reality of their situation dawned on her. "No we can't: I don't have the Key any more."

"Key?" Joe asked.

"It doesn't matter. Look, Joe, I hate to say this but I just don't think we can do it. It's a four-hour train journey down to Cardiff. You'd never make it back in time."

Joe looked back at her, wide-eyed, bewildered. Dotty could see that the hopelessness of his predicament was beginning to sink in. She felt rotten. "I know what; why don't you write them a letter and we can post it to them after..." she trailed off, her words awkward and useless. "I'll go and get some paper and a pen."

Dotty ran to her great-uncle's study, feet going as fast as they could take her, stumbling, falling, tears streaming down her face. Without knocking she burst into the room, not caring whether it was her great uncle or Strake who greeted her. "I need some writing paper - right now," she blurted.

It was Great Uncle Winchester who looked up from his seat at the writing desk. "Writing paper, you say?"

"Yes, it's for Joe. Oh, Winnie, surely there must be something we can do!"

"My dear, we have been through all this," began Great Uncle Winchester gently. "Believe me, darling girl, if there was anything I or the Council could do, we would do it gladly. I know you've been looking for an answer in the library, and I too have had my people searching day and night for a way out of this. But the simple fact of the matter is that a faerie's bargain cannot be undone. In truth it was unusual for the hob to be so generous as to give the boy time to say good-bye."

"Generous!" Dotty spat out. "There's nothing generous about it. It's just plain unfair. And with the locket gone, Joe can't even chimney hop to go and say goodbye to his parents. The whole thing is hideous. Oh, it's all my fault," she sobbed.

As Her great uncle tried in vain to comfort her, there was a gentle knock at the open door. It was Gobby.

"I'm sorry to trouble you, sir, but it's the girl, Sarah. I think it's time."

"All right, Mrs Gobbins, thank you. Dotty, do you want to go with Mrs Gobbins and say goodbye?"

"Goodbye? But what about Joe?" Dotty argued bitterly. "What about him? Shouldn't he be able to say good-bye, too?"

"Dear girl, I assure, I do understand," her great-uncle answered kindly. "But we have to accept this as one situation we cannot change. Here, let me get you some writing paper." He foraged in his desk for paper and an envelope. "Take it up with you when you go to Sarah," he continued. "The writing will help your friend. It is all we can do for now."

"Then you think there may still be a chance? To help Joe, I mean?"

"I would never wish to give you false hope, my dear. But hope exists in every situation, does it not? No matter how bad things seem. You never know, something might still turn up." Her great uncle gave her a fond kiss and sent her on her way.

Feeling a little better from her great uncle's pep talk, Dotty spent most of the afternoon with Joe, although she wasn't doing very well at making conversation on account of her repeatedly racking her brains for a solution that she just couldn't seem to find. Finally, in need of a break, she nipped down to her bedroom to skype Sylv. Dotty knew that Sylv would have wanted to see Joe, but she didn't want him any more upset than he already was. As Sylv's despair was bound to be colourful, she thought it best to save Joe from it.

When Dotty returned to the nursery, Gobby had ventured down to the oddly-quiet kitchen to prepare more food for supper, leaving Joe and Sarah alone. Joe had finished his letter and was looking pretty shaky.

"It's done," he said. "Would you?" he handed the letter to Dotty. "Oh, Dotty, I'm scared."

"Joe, I'm so sorry about all of this." Dotty embraced him, sobbing.

There was a chill breeze through the open sash, billowing the nets. Dotty turned to see the sun setting on the horizon. And then the fading red light was replaced by a blue glow. The hob was at the window.

For a moment Dotty almost didn't recognise it, such was the transformation it had undergone from the shrivelled brown creature that had brought the fateful message from Joe. It was difficult not to be in awe of the hob's beauty now, its slender frame delicate as glass, lit up from within by its fierce presence. Dotty gasped.

The hob wasted no time with niceties. "Joe, it is time," it greeted him with its silvery voice.

Dotty stood, putting herself between Joe and the hob. "You're not going to take him. I won't let you," she said defiantly. But before the hob had the chance to reply, another voice came from across the room. It was Sarah.

The little girl's eyes had flickered awake when the hob entered the room, her gaze drawn to the bright light at the open window. "What is that creature?" she cried, her face full of wonder. "It is so beautiful." She addressed the hob. "Angel, are you sent to fetch me?"

"No, Sarah," Dotty replied, her voice choking. "It is no angel. It is just a hob."

"A hob?" she smiled. "My brother caught a hob once. Found it sitting by the fireside warming its toes, he did. Picked it up just like that. His master said it was him what caught it, but it wasn't. It was Skitter."

The hob seemed enraged at the little girl's revelation. Its iridescent glow burned white hot with its anger, the bright light searing the room. Dotty had to shade her eyes. Why ever was it so angry, Dotty wondered?

"So you are the sister of the thief, Skitter?" asked the hob, its gaze piercing.

"Yes I am. Do you know him, faerie?" asked the little girl.

Suddenly Dotty realised with horror that, although innocent of the fact, Sarah had been talking about the creature's own capture. Now she was truly scared, both for the girl and for Joe.

The hob smiled an icy smile. "I gather from your greeting that you do not wish me to take your friend to the land of the Fae?" It asked Dotty.

"Of course not," she replied, fearful of what the creature might say.

"But I made a bargain for a child, did I not? That is what I am owed."

"Yes," Dotty replied, warily.

"What if I were to say to you that the bargain could be met without my taking your friend?" the hob asked. "Why don't I take another child instead? Sarah, for example. She has said she wants to go with me, after all."

"She thought you were an angel when she said that." Dotty argued, shocked.

"Anyway, you can't do it." Joe joined in. "You said so before. The bargain is with me, not her."

The hob paused momentarily, and it seemed to Dotty that everyone in the room had stopped breathing.

"I have no objections," it replied slowly, "to doing you the favour of taking the girl in Joe's stead. And yet you resist? You surprise me."

"How could I let her go in my place?" said Joe. "It would be wrong."

"She's too little. She doesn't understand." wailed Dotty.

"You humans and your petty emotions," the hob sneered. "But Joe *is* right," it continued. "The girl has not bargained with me. And so the exchange must be with her agreement. What say you, Sarah, will you go with me willingly?" it shimmered. "I could free you of your earthly bonds. Take you to a place where there is no pain, no misery. You would never grow old. Never feel hunger or cold ever again."

"Oh, yes," Sarah begged. "Please let me go instead." she struggled, trying to sit herself up to better see the creature.

"Then it is done." The glow around the hob intensified, giving way to a blue mist that hung in the room like a stray cloud.

"No!" cried Dotty once more.

"Please," begged Joe. But it was no use.

The mist started to clear, revealing a forest glade that hung in the air, shimmering like a picture caught behind glass in the sunlight. With one great effort, the girl swung her poor twisted legs from the side of the bed, her nightdress revealing the crude metal calipers which supported them.

Dotty turned to Sarah. "Please!" she begged, grabbing her, willing her to stay. "Don't go with it! You don't know what it means."

Very tenderly, the tiny girl unwound Dotty's arms from around her. "Apart from my brother, Skitter, you here in this room are the only friends I have ever known. You are so kind and I am sorry to leave you."

Dotty made to argue but Sarah shushed her with a small hand to her lips. "Dotty," she soothed. "You know that I will die if I stay here with you. And I will starve or die of cold if I return to the world of sweeps." The little girl continued amid Dotty's sobs. "But if I go with this faerie, I will be kept safe and well forever. I will never know the cold or the wind or the icy rain again."

There was colour in her cheeks now. "Thank you, Joe," she said, "for letting me take your place. I will not forget what you have done for me." Then she addressed Dotty once more. "Dotty, please tell Skitter I love him." Slowly and steadily she stood up and took a step towards the light.

Dotty let out a desperate cry. She moved away from Dotty, their hands at first still gently entwined. But at last only their fingertips were touching, and with a final sob Dotty let her go.

Sarah smiled and turned towards the mist. As she stepped into the light it seemed to fill her, breathing its essence into every part of her being; giving her strength and purpose. Dotty and Joe watched as the hollowness of her cheeks filled and her hobbling turned to walking, the cruel calipers falling away from her legs as she went farther into the forest.

As Sarah followed the faerie away into the mist, the strange ethereal landscape started to fade, the unearthly blue cloud diminishing in size, smaller and smaller, as they disappeared into the distance.

Then, at the very last moment, when there was almost nothing left to see of its magical world, the hob stopped and turned. "Funny," it said to Dotty. "This is the second time of late that I have met a human of value. You are one that is brave and strong: just like your friend Joe, here. I bid you keep him safe," it instructed.

"But I am just a girl," said Dotty hopelessly.

"To the contrary, you are a guardian. This is what you are meant to do," it said, and disappeared into the mist.

"What did it mean by that?" Dotty asked, as the blue light reached the size of a pinprick and then snuffed out, breaking the spell and leaving the room in darkness, but for the light of the fire.

There was a rap at the door and Pip poked his head around the door jamb, looking uncommonly serious. "Do you mind a visitor?" he said. "Hang on, where's Sarah?"

Dotty waved him into the room. "Typical. You've missed all the action," she said. "Sit yourself down and we'll tell you everything."

As Pip closed the door behind him an almighty shriek rang through the house. It was Gobby. "My ovens!" she cried. "My blessed ovens are back!"

Pip and Dotty grinned at each other. "That'll be the glamour wearing off, then," said Pip.

"Maybe," said Dotty. "Or maybe a friend broke it for us."

"A friend?"

"Well, perhaps not quite a friend."

"Come on Joe," said Dotty. "We need to get you home. Let's go and find Great Uncle Winchester."

"Can we go via the kitchens?" asked Joe. "I'm starving."

"Sure," said Dotty. "Gobby is bound to be cooking up a storm by now."

"I'm just going to check on a couple of things. I'll catch up with you later, Dotty." said Pip.

"Okay, but don't be too long," Dotty wagged a finger at him.

"Promise," he replied, giving her his best smile.

Dotty ushered Joe out of the room, leaving Pip lingering by the fire.

"I'm so glad you're okay," she said, giving her friend a small squeeze as they walked along.

"What's a guardian?" he asked.

"A guardian?"

"Yes. The hob called you a guardian. What did it mean?"

"I'm really not sure," admitted Dotty.

But one thing was for sure. She intended to find out.

Partings

ABOUT THE AUTHOR

Emma Warner-Reed is a qualified lawyer, academic, legal journalist and author. Emma also has her own children's book review channel on YouTube: DOTTY about BOOKS, which recommends the best reads in picture books, early/young independent readers and children's chapter books. Emma lives in a rural setting on the edge of the Yorkshire Dales with her husband, four small children and a plethora of animals, some of whom are more domesticated than others!

To date the first book in the series, DOTTY and the Calendar House Key, released in 2015, has received significant acclaim including the Literary Classics Silver Award for children's fantasy fiction, an exclusively five star rating on Amazon, the official Seal of Approval from Literary Classics and Honorable Mentions at the Los Angeles, New York, Amsterdam and Paris Book Festival Awards.

DOTTY and the Chimney Thief is the second novel in The DOTTY Series. Look out for Dotty's third adventure, DOTTY and the Dream Catchers, coming soon!

Please feel free to contact Emma for interviews, quotes or comments about her writing via any of the methods listed on the contact page on the website. For regular news, reviews and updates on The DOTTY Series, subscribe to the DOTTY mailing list at www.thedottyseries.com, or follow Emma on Twitter or Facebook.

What people have to say about DOTTY:

"Author Emma Warner-Reed has penned a magnificent children's book with suspense that builds as young readers are drawn into the mystery surrounding Dotty's new home. Dotty and the Calendar House Key is highly recommended for home and school libraries and has earned the Literary Classics Seal of Approval."

Literary Classics Book Reviews
Amazon

"Dotty and the Calendar House Key has truly fired my daughter's imagination for the first time since Harry Potter. Beautifully written and exciting. The Secret Garden meets Diagon Alley. Fabulous!"

Alexandra Vere
Harrogate

"I really liked the [first] book. It was a bit scary when Dotty found herself in Uncle Winchester's private study. But most of the books I read are a bit scary so that was okay. I would read the other books in the series. Go Team Dotty!"

Betty, age 7
Amazon

"My son has just read the first [book] and thinks it's brilliant - high praise since he has very decided opinions about what he reads."

P. Uglow
Harrogate

"Enchanting, innocent and lovely with just the right amount of modern technology...a great read for a grown up 7 year old! She loved it... When is the next one coming out?"

A. Little
Amazon

"I read [the first chapter] to the children tonight and they were instantly back to being as gripped as they were by the first book. They both laughed out loud at the wonderful descriptions of Gobby in the kitchen covered in flour (again) and the way she asked Kenny to remove Geoff! They cannot wait to find out what happens next."

J. Johnson
Stallingborough

Look out for Dotty's next adventure,
DOTTY and the Dream Catchers
coming soon!

ACKNOWLEDGMENTS

Thank you, as ever, to my lovely little family for supporting me through the writing process, and to my literary colleagues who have inspired and encouraged me along the way. In particular I would like to thank Team DOTTY, namely: Nancy Butts, who has been both an inspiration and a joy, Sarah and Isla Hannett, Ragan, Leo and Matilda Montgomery, Katherine and Annabel Czolba-Wass, Hayley and Adam Roberts (and bump), Alex and Bella Vere, Patrick, Edward and William Anderson, Belinda and Megan Brown, Tricia and Molly Redshaw, Louise Styan, Jane, Connor and Kara Johnson, Bethany Armstrong, Monica Rondino, Neera Sawhney, Rachel and Esme Libera and Cathy and Helena Kitchingman. Also Paul Douglas Lovell, for helping me with those typos, and fellow author, Marc Remus, who has been a constant ray of sunshine and reminded me what tenacity and dedication really look like.

But most importantly thank you to everyone who has bought and read the first book in the DOTTY series and who has encouraged (and even urged!) me to finish the second. A writer is nothing without their audience and so to you I offer my sincerest gratitude. Thank you for securing DOTTY's place in the literary world. I hope she and her friends continue to entertain you and many more people in the future.